D0046783

Ask Amy Green

BOY TROUBLE

Ask Amy Green

BOY TROUBLE

SARAH WEBB

CANDLEWICK PRESS

This book is dedicated to:

Robert Dunbar, for welcoming me into the children's book
world when I was a lowly bookseller in Waterstone's,

Paul Baggaley, who probably has no idea how much
he changed my life by giving me the job in the first place,

and finally to Sam, my brilliant son, who made me
stop dreaming and start writing.

This is a work of fiction. Names, characters, places, and incidents are either
products of the author's imagination or, if real, are used fictitiously.

Copyright © 2009 by Sarah Webb

All rights reserved. No part of this book may be reproduced, transmitted,
or stored in an information retrieval system in any form or by any means,
graphic, electronic, or mechanical, including photocopying, taping, and
recording, without prior written permission from the publisher.

First U.S. edition 2010

Library of Congress Cataloging-in-Publication Data
Webb, Sarah.
Ask Amy Green : boy trouble / Sarah Webb. — 1st U.S. ed.
p.   cm.
Summary: A thirteen-year-old Irish girl who helps her seventeen-year-old aunt
write an advice column for lovelorn girls faces her own dilemma when she
alienates her friends after falling for a cute but aloof boy in her art class.
ISBN 978-0-7636-5006-3
[1. Advice columns — Fiction. 2. Dating (Social customs) — Fiction.
3. Aunts — Fiction. 4. Ireland — Fiction.]   I. Title.
PZ7.W3838As 2010
[Fic] — dc22   2009049041

10 11 12 13 14 15 16   RRC   10 9 8 7 6 5 4 3 2 1

Printed in Crawfordsville, IN, U.S.A.

This book was typeset in ITC Giovanni.

Candlewick Press
99 Dover Street
Somerville, Massachusetts 02144

visit us at www.candlewick.com

Hi there,

Welcome to the first Ask Amy Green book.

Thanks so much for picking it up. I'd like to tell you a little about myself before you start reading. Or, if you like, jump right in and read this later.

I'm so excited to have American readers. Like Amy Green, I loooove America. I have relatives and friends all over the States — Denver (Aunt Dorothy and Uncle Gully), Washington, D.C., (cousin John), Boston (cousin Emily), L.A. (second cousin Susan), Connecticut (best friend, Denise) — there are loads more but you get the drift. I'm off to Washington, D.C., soon to check out the National Gallery and catch up with my fave cousin. I can't wait! I'm a huge art fan and John is so much fun to hang out with.

Like Amy Green, I'm Irish through and through. I live in Dun Laoghaire, which is a difficult to pronounce (you say "Dun Leery") but very lovely seaside town near Dublin city, the capital of Ireland.

I have three children: Sam, 16; Amy, 7 (Amy Green is named after her); and Jago, 4. They provide lots of inspiration, especially my son and his friends with all their romantic entanglements. Oops, sorry — Sam says I'm embarrassing him again.

This book was also inspired by some real Irish teenagers, including my special teen advisor and editor, Kate Gordon. And also my own teen diaries. In fact, many of things that happen in the book have also happened to real people, me included. Like when Amy meets the utterly Swoon-ville Seth on Killiney beach and they . . . Well, you'll just have to read on and find out!

And watch out for Amy and Clover's trip to Miami in my next book, *Ask Amy Green: Summer Secrets*.

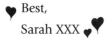 Best,
Sarah XXX

♥ Chapter 1

"Boys!" Clover taps a pink gel pen against her top teeth, making a hollow rattling noise. "They never change. What idiots!"

She swivels around in her office chair and presses a button on her computer. The printer whirs into action. She hands me two pages. "Read this and weep, Amy."

> To: agonyaunt@gossmagazine.com
> Tuesday
>
> Dear Clover,
>   Please help! It's boy trouble. (What else?) I hooked up with this mega-cute guy two weeks ago at a Sinister Teen Frite Nite. But he's a year

ahead of me in school, and I have no idea where I stand.

We've been to the movies a couple of times, and he texts me a lot. But I'm confused—one minute he's all over me; the next he's completely ignoring me. What should I do? Play it cool or play along? I'm seeing him tonight. Please advise.

Anxious in Artane

(otherwise known as Wendy, 14)

To: agonyaunt@gossmagazine.com
Wednesday

Dear Clover,

I wrote to you yesterday about a boy. Well, today I found out he's been spreading nasty rumors about me in school. Saying I kiss like a washing machine! I think it's because I told him to go easy on Saturday night. I wanted to watch at least some of the movie.

I'm so embarrassed. All the boys in my class are calling me Wendy Whirlpool, and the D4 girls are all sniggering at me in the halls and spinning their fingers around in circles.

I don't know what to do. It's a nightmare. I haven't been able to eat all day. My friends are telling me to pay no attention, but I can't stop thinking about it. I feel like everyone's staring at me.

I'm going to pull a sickie tomorrow and Friday, but I'll have to go back to school on Monday.

Please help me. I'm in bits.

Morto,

Wendy

My eyes widen as I read Wendy's e-mails. I cringe inwardly. I understand exactly how she feels — sick to the stomach with worry. Feeling dozens of pairs of eyes boring into her. Paranoid, unsettled, deeply unhappy.

"What do you think?" Clover says.

"I feel sorry for the poor girl. I'd hate to be in her shoes."

"Any advice for her?"

I shrug. "To ignore everyone, I suppose, like her friends say. If it's anything like our school, it'll all blow over in a few weeks. I'd tell her to put her head down and pretend she's invisible."

Clover blows a raspberry. "*Wrong* answer!"

I stare at her. "If you're so clever, what's the right answer, then?"

"Duh! Fight back. Don't let the eejit get away with it."

That does sound far more interesting. But it's hardly practical. "How? Wendy doesn't sound all that confident." I squirm a little. This is all getting too close for comfort.

Clover tilts her head. "Wendy?"

"The girl in the letter." I stab the printout with my finger.

"Right, Wendy. Let me think." After a moment, her eyes light up. "Hang on. Maybe *she* doesn't have to be confident. Maybe someone else can be confident for her."

Clover smiles at me, her eyes sparkling. She's up to something. Goose pimples run up and down my spine.

"Oh, no, Clover. Don't look at *me*. I'm so not getting involved. Just answer the letter. Tell her to ignore them."

But Clover just smiles knowingly. "Amy, I've made a decision: we're not going to be *that* kind of agony aunt. We are going to give *good* advice to readers."

"We?" I stare at her.

"Yes, *we*, Beanie. You're going to help me."

"Really? Do I have a say in this?"

"Let me see." She taps her teeth with the pen again. "Ho-hum." She pretends to be thinking deeply. "No! And we're going to get very, very involved. It'll be oodles more fun, don't you think? And I'll get the agony page and maybe even an article out of it, or my name's not Clover Wildgust. I can see it now." She puts her hands in the air. "*Ta-da!* 'Teenage Boys Dissing You? How to Get Your Own Back, by Clover Wildgust.' No. Clover *M*. Wildgust. I do like a middle initial, don't you? It adds a bit of gravitas. Clover M. Wildgust. My first byline. It'll be the start of a beautiful career." Her eyes go all starry.

I put my head in my hands. Mum's right: Clover *is* delusional.

"Right, Beanie," she continues, "this Wendy business calls for drastic action. We need a killer plan."

I'm worried now. When Clover takes drastic action, it's usually just that — drastic. Like when she got bored one day and dyed her hair electric blue, or when she drove through Dublin city in her Mini Cooper with the top down in the middle of February for a dare. She was wearing a bikini at the time and got her picture in two national newspapers. Gramps wasn't amused.

Clover stares at the bulletin board in front of her

desk. I follow her gaze. It's chock-full of all kinds of invitations: to book launches, beauty nights, fashion shows, and parties. My eyes flit past them and rest on the luminous green invitation. You can't miss it — in gothic writing, it screams:

Dance the Night Away at Sinister Teen Frite Nite

Sinister FM's Teen Frite Nites are famous. They're on every Friday at Monkstown Rugby Club, and they're strictly for under sixteens, with no alcohol. Anyone who's anyone goes to them. My friends Mills and Sophie are always trying to drag me along. I've been a couple of times, but it's always so packed and I hate dancing in front of people. I get all self-conscious. Then my stomach knots up, and I feel sick and want to go home. Besides, it's always jammers with D4s and Crombies; it's like their weekly cattle market for new boyfriends and girlfriends.

D4s are girls who live or would like to live in Dublin 4, a posh area of Dublin. They wear Ugg boots with skinny jeans or minis and are addicted to fake tans and hair straighteners.

Crombies are their male equivalents. The play rugby, wear Abercrombie & Fitch and other designer gear, and say "ledge" (short for *legend*) a lot. In Ireland, they are the closest thing we have to Neanderthal men, and D4s find them wildly attractive. Figures!

"Grab that green invitation for me," Clover says.

I pass it to her, and she turns it over. "Hey, Beanie, would I pass for a fourteen-year-old?"

I look at her carefully. What's she up to?

"Well?" she asks again.

I bite my lip, considering. Clover is on the small side, with the kind of straight, white-blond hair you usually find on a Bratz doll. It's so long she can almost sit on it, and when it's windy, it sticks to her lip gloss. Clover's hair is real, but the color's most certainly not. Gramps says it'll fall out if she keeps bleaching it, but she just ignores him.

Today she's wearing a mouse-gray Juicy tracksuit teamed with a white sequined tank. Her flip-flopped feet are resting on the large wooden desk, her petal-like toenails a warm peachy color. She looks a little too knowing for a fourteen-year-old, too comfortable in her skin. Plus she refuses to wear Ugg boots, says they give her sweaty feet.

I shrug. "Maybe. On a dark night."

"It'll be dark, all right." She smiles and her china-blue eyes twinkle dangerously. "I have a plan. We're not going to let boys behave like eejits anymore. We're going to take revenge. For Wendy." She waves her arms around excitedly. "For teenage girls every-where. But I'm gonna need you, and your sweaty yeti boots."

♥ Chapter 2

Before we go any further, let me explain how I got sucked into the whole agony aunt business in the first place.

Clover recently landed a job on teen magazine the *Goss* during her gap year between school and college. It's kind of like *Seventeen* or *CosmoGirl* but with more articles and less celebrity pics. Not many Irish celebs actually live in Ireland; they mostly hang out in Hollywood, like swoon-boy Colin Farrell and the utterly gorge Cork lad with the big lips, Jonathan Rhys Meyers.

The mag's paying her and everything. She wants to be a journalist, so it's great experience. Gramps set it up; he knows the editor's dad. The agony aunt had just gone on maternity leave, so Clover asked could she give it a go. To her surprise, they said yes. Clover thinks they were probably a bit desperate.

I overheard Mum talking to Dave, her boyfriend (I refuse to call him my stepdad — it's too Cinderella. Besides, they're not married or anything, but more about that later). "Clover is so lucky," she said. "Things always seem to land in her lap." It must seem that way to Mum, but Clover works really hard when she wants to. Which, in fairness, isn't all that often.

You should also know:

1. Clover has always been spoiled, according to Mum. Mum and Clover are sisters, and they have a bit of a love/hate relationship. I guess it's because of the age difference — twenty years!

2. Clover's seventeen going on thirteen (my age), which is probably why we click so well. Technically she's my aunt, but we're more like sisters.

3. Clover is very popular with boys and is always stringing some poor guy or other along. At the moment, it's Ryan, who's studying humanities at Trinity, an ancient college in Dublin with cobblestones and

big metal sculptures worth millions just sitting outside on the grass.

4. Clover lives at home with her dad, my grampa, or "Gramps," as we both call him. I couldn't say "Grampa" when I was little, only "Cramps" and then "Gramps." Clover used to call him "Gramps" in a baby voice to annoy him, then it just stuck.

5. Clover's currently on what she has decided will be the first of many gap years from studying or working full-time. She has it all figured out!

She has a place to study humanities at Trinity College (like Ryan) but deferred for a year. The Leaving Certificate almost put her off academia for life, she says. She did surprisingly well in her final exams for someone whose idea of studying is cramming the night before.

Clover also says she intends to live at home for years and years so she can spend all her money on the important things in life, like clothes, shoes, and going out. Clover is no fool, according to Mum. But Gramps has just retired, and he likes having Clover around the place — he says she livens things up. Clover says she keeps him young; Mum says she's delusional and that her shenanigans will send him to an early grave.

6. Clover doesn't mince her words. Mum says she's borderline rude; Clover says she's just honest. If you ask me, the truth lies somewhere in between.

7. Oh, and she's crazy about elephants.

After school on Wednesday, Clover rang me in a complete tizzy.

"I've been reading some of the 'Dear Clover' letters," she said. "You think you lot have problems, try paying for petrol. I haven't bought shoes in weeks. One or two of them are worth answering, but most of them, *ooh-la-la!*" — she made a yawning noise — "boring. Someone asked me the answer to a percentages problem, as if I'd know. Ha!" She snorted.

"Hi, Amy. How are you?" I said sarcastically, after she'd finished ranting on about the dull and pointless letters for a few more minutes. And to be fair to Clover, some of them were total Yawnsville. "How's school? Any news? Sorry I haven't rung in an age. Can I take you shopping to make up for it?"

She gave a deep sigh. "Don't you start, Beanie. Your mother's bad enough. Listen, I need your help."

"Oh?" This wasn't exactly a new one to me. Usually it means lending her some of my hard-earned babysitting money. Clover is permanently broke, even though she is the one working, now on the magazine, previously at a grocery checkout. (She used to put on funny accents to amuse herself—American, German, and Polish. She is brilliant at accents.) She is a complete shopaholic and spends every cent she earns with the speed of Usain Bolt. Luckily that includes spending money on li'l ol' me!

"You're a first-year, right?" she asked.

"Last time I looked."

"So you know how their petty little minds work."

"Petty? Hey!"

"I should have said insignificant."

"Do you want my help or not?"

"Look, I'll come straight to the point. I've found someone with a proper problem to fix. It's such a sad e-mail; her ex-boyfriend's behaving like a complete pig, surprise, surprise. I feel really sorry for her. But I have no idea what to tell her. Help me, Beanie. Please? It's my first agony aunt page, and I really want to impress Saffy." Saffy is her editor. She sounds a bit scary, like a head teacher.

"What's your deadline?" I knew all the jargon from listening to Clover over the last few weeks. The deadline is basically the day you have to hand your article, or "piece," in to the editor. When you've e-mailed it, you've "filed copy." The "byline" is just your name at the top of the piece — "by Amy Green" in my case.

"Yesterday," she said. Clover always leaves everything till the last minute. Two years ago, she went on holiday with me and Mum to Rome, and we came very close to missing the flight because of her. When we arrived to collect her in the taxi, she couldn't find her passport. Mum was not amused. She refused to speak to Clover in the cab, giving her dark looks and glancing at her watch, while tut-tutting every few minutes and muttering about being late for your own funeral. I was stuck between them like a slice of ham in a sandwich, and it wasn't a pleasant experience.

In the end we had to sprint to the gate. We were the last on the plane by miles, and all the other passengers gave us filthy looks as we walked down the aisle with glowing faces, puffing and panting. We delayed the flight by twenty minutes, and they weren't happy. They only held it at all because Clover flirted outrageously with one of the guards at the security screening. She told him she was a swimsuit model and had a photo shoot in Rome that very afternoon, and could he be an absolute pet and help her or she'd miss the flight. He phoned the gate and begged them to keep it open for a few more minutes. Clover deserved an Oscar for her effort. Even Mum was impressed.

Clover gave a huge breathy sigh through the phone. "Saffy's given me until tomorrow morning." She made an *AAAGHHH* noise that sounded like the fast spin of a washing machine.

I was amazed. It wasn't like Clover to get so stressed.

"Beanie," she begged, "I really, really need your help. Are you busy? Can you come over? Like now?"

Busy? I was pacing the kitchen, trying to soothe my three-month-old baby sister, Evie, who was strapped across my front in a rainbow tie-dyed baby sling. I was simultaneously watching my little brother, Alex, trying to feed his wooden ABC blocks into the ancient VCR that Mum had rescued from the closet under the stairs and resurrected. Alex had broken the DVD player a week ago by ripping the DVD tray out: he was more troll than toddler. Mum was on an emergency milk and nappies run, leaving me holding the fort.

"Just keep them alive," Mum had said as she'd flown out the door.

No, not busy at all!

"I'm babysitting," I said smugly. I prodded Evie in the hope she'd give a little wail to prove I was telling the truth, but she'd finally dropped off to sleep.

"Where's Sylvie? Has she finally run off? Wouldn't blame her, with you lot."

"No! Of course not. She's just coming in the door. I'll ring you back." Mum walked toward me, dumped her heavily laden Tesco shopping bag on the floor, and threw her keys onto the kitchen counter with a clatter.

"Sorry, sorry." Her cheeks were flushed pink, and I didn't think she'd washed her hair for days, let alone brushed it. There was a white milky stain on the shoulder of her sky-blue fleece, and she looked wrecked. She held out her arms to take Evie off me. While she supported Evie's weight, I untangled myself from the sling—David Blaine, eat your heart out.

When I was finally free, I said, "Mum, Clover just rang. She said she'll help me with my math homework if I come over."

"Did she really?" Mum squinted at me a little suspiciously. It was a first. Clover didn't believe in homework. She said it was a complete waste of time and energy.

I nodded eagerly. "Yes. It's algebra."

Mum winced. Math wasn't her strong point. Alex threw a block across the room, and it banged at our feet, waking Evie up. She opened her tiny mouth and howled like a banshee.

"Go." Mum put Evie over her shoulder and patted her back. "You'll never get your homework done in this madhouse. But back before dinner, OK?"

♥ Chapter 3

Fifteen minutes later, I rested my bike against Clover's "office," a wooden shed at the end of Gramps's back garden, and rapped on the door. Always best to knock with Clover — you never know what she's up to. The shed had originally been built for Gran's flower arranging. She'd been a florist for years, and after she'd retired, she had still done the flowers for the local church and the odd wedding and funeral. She'd loved flowers, had Gran, said it was in her blood.

But Gran died four years ago of breast cancer. Mum said it was a blessing; Gran had been sick for ages. But it had still been hard.

The last time I'd seen her, she'd looked really, really tired and her face had been pale and waxy, like an apple skin. She'd told me she was proud to have such a beautiful and talented granddaughter. "Never forget how special you are," she'd said, adding that I wasn't to be sad when she was gone, that she'd had a good life and had been lucky to have had time to get to know me properly.

I know she said not to, but I still get sad thinking about her. She was lovely. She always made chocolate fudge cake when I visited and never asked me about school or anything boring like that. I don't think she'd mind me being a bit sad.

Clover was only thirteen when Gran died: my age. Imagine! I don't know what I'd do if Mum died now. Clover went all quiet for weeks and weeks after the funeral. Mum was really worried about her. Sometimes Clover used to stay with us on the weekend. The three of us — me, Clover, and Mum — would curl up on the sofa, eat ice cream, and watch movies. One evening we put on this old film called *Beaches*, and Mum tried to stop it halfway through 'cause one of the characters was dying. But Clover made us watch right to the end. We all cried buckets that night. Funnily enough, after that Clover seemed a bit more like herself.

The shed is pretty amazing inside. When Clover

got the job at the *Goss*, we all pitched in to help her decorate and make it into a proper office. The walls are a nice creamy white; there are striped red, pink, and white blinds on the windows, and against one wall, there's a comfy red sofa that my dad donated from his office. It used to be in the reception area of his trading floor, where he is a big-shot trader. Even Dave joined in: he found a cool black leather office chair on eBay and drove all the way to Kildare to collect it.

Clover turned the old florist's counter into a desk, complete with laptop, printer, and a tower of primary-colored plastic in-trays, all stacked on top of one another like a horizontal version of Connect Four. As well as writing the agony aunt column, Clover also compiles the "What's Up?" pages at the front of the *Goss*, telling readers about up-and-coming launches and gigs. She brings bags of stuff home from the magazine to sift through, and her in-trays are always crammed with press releases, invitations, and free makeup and perfume samples. Every now and then, I prioritize her in-trays for her — she is hopeless at it.

Today Clover's desk was littered with sheets of printed paper, a thick rubber band the color of surgical bandages, half-used gel pens (mostly pink), Gramps's dog-eared *Oxford English Dictionary* (my idea, since Clover's spelling is appalling), a candyfloss-pink lip gloss, the latest *Grazia* magazine, and a pair of fabby Gucci aviator sunglasses with green lenses.

"New?" I asked, picking them up. They were surprisingly heavy.

"Yep. One of the perks of the job. We did a feature on sunglasses and picked them as our 'In Trend' glasses for the summer. The Gucci distributor sent each of us a free pair. Score! Apparently they've nearly sold out in Ireland already. Power of the press, Beanie. Power of the press."

"Can I try them on?"

"Sure."

I lowered them over my eyes. The world turned a lush, mossy green. They channeled coolness. "Wow! Thanks, Clover. I'll cherish them forever."

She put her hand out, palm up. "Hand them over, Bean Machine. You can have my old pink ones. Now, let's get down to business."

That was when she handed me Wendy's e-mail.

"So are you in, Beanie? Will you help me?" Clover asks. "Go on." She smiles at me. "Please? It'll be fun."

It's very difficult to say no to Clover. I give a mock sigh. "Oh, I suppose so. It's got to be better than homework."

She jumps up and gives me a smacker on the lips. I wipe them with the back of my hand. "Yuck! Clover!" She just laughs. And against my better judgment, I help her formulate a plan of action.

Clover's enthusiasm is highly infectious. Mum says she could talk Inuits into buying snow. I always get swept along by the sheer force of her will. And let's be honest — I'm dying to see just how far she'll go. I know Mum will kill me if she ever finds out I've been cooking up crazy revenge schemes with Clover, and as for Dave, he'll go ballistic.

Dave never used to be such a boring old crusty. In fact, when I first met him, he was great fun. He used to let me bang on his bongo drums, and he even showed me how to play some old Beatles songs on his guitar. He was in this band years ago called the Colts, and they nearly made it, according to Mum. After the band split up, Dave used to sing and play his guitar in pubs, but he hasn't done that since the babies came along.

At the moment, I can't do a thing right in his eyes. It's all "Amy, have you done your homework?" and "Amy, can you keep an eye on Evie?" Amy this, Amy that. Aagh!

And in a way that's also why I decide to help

Clover. To get up Dave's long, angular nose. He thinks he's so cool, in his T-shirts with obscure bands on them and his iPod that holds thousands of songs, but he's not. He has a wobbly stomach, and one of his fingers is all bendy and funny-looking from playing the guitar so much; plus he has a huge mouth that you could fit a dinner plate into, sideways. And he's practically bald. Ah yes, he has it all going for him. Mum thinks he looks like a young Mick Jagger. As if.

Suddenly Clover gets all businesslike, and I try to keep a straight face. I love Clover in serious mode; she turns into the boss from *The Devil Wears Prada*. If I didn't know her so well, I'd be completely intimidated. As it is, I'm trying not to laugh. I watch her as she scribbles on a notebook in her spidery handwriting.

"First we need more information," she barks. "I want you to e-mail Wendy and ask her the following questions. Pretend to be me." She rips the page out of her notebook and hands it to me.

I read her list (I'm used to her handwriting), my nose scrunching up. "Clover, we're supposed to be giving her advice, not asking her questions. And why do you need the boy's name and address?"

"No questions, Grasshopper," she says in a terrible ninja accent. She jumps to her feet. "I just need to nip out to the joke shop."

"The what?"

"All will be revealed." She winks at me mysteriously and thrusts her hands into her pockets. They come out empty. "*Siúcra!* Got any spondulicks?"

Siúcra — Irish for sugar — is Clover's second fave saying after "Got any spondulicks?" I hand her a crumpled ten-euro note, the last of my babysitting money. "It's a loan, Clover. I want it back. And I thought you wanted an adviser, not a secretary," I say to her disappearing back. "How will I explain all this to Wendy?"

"You're smart, Bean Machine," she says without turning around. "You'll think of something."

I sit down at her desk and click open the Internet. So much for my math homework. I'll have to do it later. Luckily I'm good at algebra.

I wiggle my fingers around and then place them on the compact and slightly sticky keyboard of Clover's laptop. I taught myself to type the summer Alex was born, when Dave gave me an old computer from work. He's a nurse at Saint Vincent's Hospital. A *nurse*, can you believe it? How embarrassing.

"A present from the baby." He laughed.

"We won't be able to take you out much this summer," Mum explained. "We thought you could write a journal or something."

Mum's into writing. Before she had Alex, she was a scriptwriter for *Fair City*, Ireland's answer to *EastEnders*. She had every intention of going back after her maternity leave, had a day care lined up and everything, but then bang, Evie came along. It would have cost too much to put both of them into day care, so Mum's stuck at home.

"I'm hardly Anne Frank," I told her. "What have I got to write about? Baby poo that looks like mustard? How to use a sterilizer?" She just smiled at me gently and said, "That would be lovely, pet." She hadn't really been listening. Mothers are quite, quite crazy, especially when they've just had a baby.

Dear Wendy, I type slowly and carefully. I have to watch my fingers while I type, but I can do twenty-seven words a minute, with very few mistakes.

This is Clover from the *Goss*. Thank you for your e-mail. I'm so sorry you're having such problems at school and with that boy. He sounds like a nasty piece of work.

I stop for a second. That's a bit old-fashioned, like something you'd read in a book. I delete it. *He sounds like a complete eejit,* I write instead. *I would certainly like to help you.*

> In order to give you the best possible advice, I have a few questions. Your answers will be strictly confidential, but I guarantee that if all goes well, come Monday morning, *he'll* be the one everyone's gossiping about.
>
> I have a plan. You mentioned Sinister Frite Nites. . . .

"Any luck?" Clover asks when she gets back. She plonks a large canary-yellow paper bag down on the desk and flops onto her sofa.

I reach out to open the bag, but she swats my hand away.

"All in good time." She picks up the bag and puts it into her filing cabinet, then turns the tiny key and tucks it into her pink padded bra. She readjusts the lacy bra straps, pulling them up a little to give her cleavage more oomph.

"Go on, spill," she says.

"If you stop fiddling with your bra straps, I'll tell you."

"Ooooh! What's eating you? At least I have boobs."

"Thanks for making me feel even better about my pancake chest."

She grabs at the neck of my T-shirt and peers down.

"Clover!" I pull away. I rearrange my stretched T-shirt. "Do you mind? This happens to be my favorite top. If it doesn't go back into shape, I'll kill you."

"It's a plain black T-shirt."

"I just like it, OK?" I say a little huffily. Clover has no sense of personal space or boundaries.

"You need a proper bra, Beanie. We'll go shopping. Sort you out. I know just the place."

"I'm a big girl now. I can do my own shopping."

She gives a snort. "Hello? You're wearing an undershirt."

"A sports bra."

She shrugs. "Same difference. You need something with a little padding. Something that gives you shape." She holds a palm out in front of her own chest. "Even I need a little help," she admits.

I shrug. She's probably right. Clover does know her underwear. She has an amazing lingerie collection and is always showing me her shopping; she loves an audience, and Mum doesn't really approve of all her spending.

Clover says, "Anyway, back to work. Where do we stand with Wendy? Any news?"

"Oh, yes." I hand her Wendy's reply.

She reads it and a smile creeps across her mouth. "Bingo." She ruffles my hair. "Good on you, Beanie. We're in business."

♥ Chapter 4

On Friday evening, Clover arrives at my house at twenty past eight.

"You're late." I scowl at her, but I don't know why I bother. Clover's always late. I think I'm just nervous.

She ignores me. "Got the Uggly boots?"

I nod and hand over my pride and joys. She takes one from me gingerly and sniffs it. She'd instructed me to spray their lining with foot deodorant and leave them outside the back door all day to freshen up.

"They'll do," she says. She takes off her flip-flops, pulls a pair of navy sports socks out of her bag, sits down on the bottom stair, and edges them carefully over her newly French-manicured toes. "I'm not taking any chances," she says. "You might have a verruca or athlete's foot or something."

I give a disgusted snort. "I don't have any fungal infections, thanks very much."

Clover just grins. She follows the socks with my Ugg boots, then stands up and takes a few steps. "I suppose they are quite comfy," she concedes. She looks me up and down, wrinkling her nose. "You look like an emo. Are *all* your clothes black?"

"No," I say defensively. I thought I looked all right. I'm wearing a black scoop-neck top, my best Diesel skinny jeans, a wide gold sparkly belt, and gold ballet flats. OK, the jeans are black too, but, hey, it's my favorite color.

She must have noticed my face drop because she says, "You look great, Beanie. And that belt really shows off your teeny waist. I didn't mean anything by it. I'm just nervous. You know what I'm like when I'm under pressure."

I certainly do. Since starting at the *Goss*, Clover seems to be living in a state of semipermanent stress. She says it comes with the job and that all journos live on the edge. Mum says Clover is a total drama queen and isn't happy unless something terrible is happening to her. For once, Mum might be on to something.

Mum walks into the hall, Evie snoozing in her arms. "Amy, back by ten thirty, OK? And make Clover drop you off at the door. Do you have your keys? Try not to wake the baby when you come in." She says all this to the top of Clover's head. She's clearly in one of her sleep-deprived dazes.

"I'm behind you," I say. "That's Clover on the stairs."

Mum jumps, making Evie cry. "Jeepers, my heart," she says, patting her chest with one hand. "I nearly dropped the baby." She croons at Evie, who gurgles a little and then goes back to sleep. "And why are you wearing Ugg boots, Clover? I thought you hated them." Mum's eyes narrow.

"Changed my mind," Clover says breezily. "Ready, Beanie? And don't worry, Sylvie — I'll drop her off at the door."

"And back by half ten, mind," Mum says.

Clover gives her a wide smile. "We're only going for pizza, Sis. Stop worrying."

Dave walks through the kitchen door. I glare at him and back toward the wall. The hall's getting a bit too crowded for my liking. He rubs his stubbly chin and yawns. "Did someone say pizza? Any chance of bringing me back a few slices?"

The man is obsessed with food. My heart sinks. Clover looks at me, her mouth distorted from biting her lip.

Luckily Mum says, "You've already had dinner, pet. Do you really need pizza too?"

"Maybe not." He gives a laugh and then puts his head on Mum's shoulder. "Must get my pre-baby figure back." He winks at her.

Mum kisses the top of his head and I cringe. I do wish they wouldn't be so lovey-dovey in front of people (me in particular); it's embarrassing.

"Love to stay and chat, but we have to run," Clover says, brushing past Mum and Dave and opening the front door. "Our reservation's for eight. And just look at the time. Come on, Beanie. Mush!"

Twenty minutes later, we park beside a Sinister FM jeep, a few meters down the road from Monkstown Rugby Club. A flock of D4 girls are sitting on the low wall opposite us, swinging their orange legs, hitting the heels of their Ugg boots against the concrete and flicking their overly styled hair for Ireland. D4s spend most of the time hanging out in town or in Dundrum Shopping Centre, when they aren't stuck in front of their mirrors straightening their hair, or slapping on fake tans. Sophie and Mills, my best friends, fancy themselves as D4s, but it's pure aspiration.

"Ready?" Clover asks me. She gloops on red lip gloss like war paint.

My stomach churns. Lots of people from my school go to the Sinister Frite Nites. Sophie tried to get me to come along tonight, but I said no, I was busy.

"Doing what?" Sophie asked, giving me a twisted smile. "Changing the skin on your Bebo page again?"

I bristled. I like my Bebo page. It's a whole heap better than either of their pages. They just use the same boring old skins and video clips and songs as everyone else. I try to be more original. But sometimes when you're thirteen, being original isn't appreciated.

"I think we should wait for a while." I stare at the D4s. They throw their heads back and hoot loudly with laughter when two emo girls walk past in striped Pippi Longstocking tights. "We don't want to look too eager."

To be honest, I'm terrified of hard-core D4s. If you look at them wrong or they spot a weakness, they'll bare their fangs and rip you to pieces with their bitchy comments, like a preppy wolf pack. And their verbal wounds can take a long time to heal. I should know; I still have the mental scars to prove it.

The first time they swooped down on me was after Mum had trimmed my fringe. She'd pulled down on it when it was damp and had cut it far too short.

The D4s followed me around, calling me "Freak Fringe" for a week. The second time was even worse. I wore Mum's padded navy raincoat to school one day — big mistake, but Mum had insisted. It was pelting down rain, I couldn't find my own jacket, and she said I'd catch pneumonia. They christened me "Amy Anorak." It lasted a whole month.

Clover nods at me. "You're right. I'm being too impatient. I guess I'm kinda nervous."

"Really?"

"Sure. This could all go horribly wrong. I could end up looking like a complete eejit." Her eyes rest on mine and then bunny-hop away. She *is* nervous. Clover Wildgust, the most confident person I know, is nervous. And if she's nervous, what hope do I have? I may as well just curl up and die right now.

"Here's the thing, Beanie," she says, reading my mind. "Everyone gets nervous sometimes. It's how you deal with it that matters. I can drive away from here right now and let that loser Brett Stokes win"— Brett is the boy from Wendy's e-mail —"or I can just swallow down the butterflies and get on with it. I have a choice."

"But what if it all goes wrong?"

"Then at least I tried. Look, I used to be just like you when I was thirteen. Nervous and self-conscious, worried that everyone was staring at me, thinking, 'Who's that loser?' "

"Honestly?"

"Sure. I was a lot better dressed obviously—"

"Hey!"

She gives me a wide grin. "Only joking. I was a complete fashion victim. Some of the photos." She shudders. "But, hey, thirteen's a rubbish age. No one ever tells you that. First year's a killer. It starts getting better in second year. And by third year, you'll be having a blast. And you have all those cute fifth- and sixth-year boys to ogle all day. That's got to be worth something."

I blush. I already have a big crush on one of the fifth-years. Simon Debrett. He's editor of the school magazine, *Saint John's News*—how original, even I could come up with a better name than that—and he's also on the firsts soccer team and the seconds rugby team, although he's no Crombie. He's actually really clever, and he doesn't mind showing it.

He takes my field hockey team, the Minor A's, for fitness training. Often he takes pity on me and lets me sit out some of the laps 'cause I have to do them in my goalie pads. Our coach, Miss Gibbons, is really tough, but we got into the semifinals of the cup last season, so she must be doing something right.

Simon held the locker-room door open for me once, and I've never forgotten it. He's dreamy. Sometimes I watch him at rugby or soccer practice when I'm in art. The art studio looks out onto the playing fields, and I just can't help myself. If I'm having a really bad day, just a tiny glimpse of his muscular thighs in his muddy shorts cheers me up to no end.

I told Mills about my crush, and she told Sophie. And now when he passes us in the hallway, Sophie always elbows me and says, "There's your boyfriend." Once she even pushed me into him. I was so humiliated. He must think I'm such an idiot. I try to avoid him now. Funnily enough, he still says hi to me sometimes. As I said, he's a nice guy.

We sit in the car and watch dozens of boys walk into Monkstown Rugby Club. Based on Wendy's careful description, none of them is Brett Stokes. She said he always arrives after nine, an hour late — he thinks it makes him look cool. It's only just nine, so we can't have missed him. We study four new Crombie boys who are strutting toward the D4s.

"Hang on a sec," Clover says. "Look at that guy with the blond highlights. And he's the right height. Do you think it's Brett?" The boys are all wearing hoodies or designer tops and Dubes, just like in

Wendy's notes. The tallest one — the one with the perfect highlights — is swaggering toward the girls.

I quickly buzz down the tinted window of Clover's Mini Cooper convertible. It used to be Gran's. She won it in a supermarket competition, of all things. Clover did her driving test as soon as she hit seventeen, passed first time too.

"Hey, Brett," one of the D4s calls out.

"Bingo," Clover says. "I can smell bacon a mile away. Oink, oink."

I shush her, trying to listen in.

Brett says, "Hey, Charlene, looking good."

The girl called Charlene flicks her hair and simpers, "Thanks."

"Yeah, for a dog." He holds his hand up and does a high five with one of his mates.

The other girls titter nervously, and the boys walk off singing "Who Let the Dogs Out?" and barking at one another.

Charlene is left glaring at his back, lobster-faced. The other girls huddle around her, like a rugby team, commiserating, telling her what a creep he is. They're probably thanking their lucky stars that they kept their mouths firmly shut.

"That's our man." Clover looks at me. "Ready, Beanie?"

"Ready as I'll ever be."

As we walk past the D4s, who are now back to kicking their legs on the wall as if Brett had never happened, they giggle.

"Nice boots," one of them says and sniggers. "So last season."

Clover swings around. "Are you talking to me?" She puts her hands on her hips and glares the girl down.

"Um, no," the girl says timidly. Clover can look quite fierce when she narrows her eyes. In fact, she looks just like Mum.

"Good," Clover says. "And you should exfoliate before you fake-tan. Your legs are all blotchy. You'll never get even coverage unless you have a smooth surface to work with."

The girl looks confused.

Clover just walks off, tut-tutting to herself. "Those D4s, thick as tree trunks most of them. And do they have to use beach spades to trowel on their makeup? Yuck."

I smile at her. Maybe this evening isn't going to be quite so bad after all. But then I spy Sophie and Mills in the queue. Oops, they'll kill me. I should have told them I was coming. I try ducking behind Clover, but it's too late; they've seen me.

"You're my friend, right?" I whisper to Clover. "Not my aunt."

"Sure, Beanie. Whatever." She shrugs. "But isn't that Mills? She knows exactly who I am. And who's that with her? It's not the infamous Sophie?"

I nod. I've told Clover a little bit about Sophie, namely that she's a wannabe D4 and that her favorite hobbies are moaning about everything and picking on people, me and Mills included.

Clover squeezes my shoulder and leans in toward me. "I'm well able to handle a Sophie, Beanie. Bring it on."

As we walk toward the queue, I feel sick. If it wasn't for Clover, I'd run away. I don't know what to do with my hands — they're shaking like Jell-O — so I shove them into the pockets of my jeans.

Clover smooths down her tiny denim shorts and strides directly toward Mills and Sophie. She has amazingly toned legs; if I didn't know better, I'd say she spent hours in the gym every day. I follow behind her, feeling like Cinderella *before* her fairy godmother's help.

Clover spins around and winks at me. Everyone in the queue is staring at her, especially the boys. Only then do I feel a bubble of excitement in my stomach. With Clover as wingman, I feel safe, proud, and even a tiny bit confident. People probably think we're best friends or something—how cool is that?

But we're related, I think suddenly, *not friends, and Clover is only here because of her* Goss *job.* Then I sink back down to earth with a bump, all excitement gone. I begin to feel nervous and plain again.

"Smile, Beanie," Clover says. "Pretend you're feeling on top of the world. That's what I always do. Breathe in positive energy. Radiate confidence from your solar plexus." She grins. "I read that in the magazine last week. Good, isn't it?"

"But what does it mean?"

She giggles. "No idea."

Instead of breathing in positive energy, I touch the back of Clover's hair and say a little prayer. Whoever's up there, if you're listening, please give me just a smidgen of Clover's confidence.

Then I plaster a grin on my face and pretend I'm having the time of my life.

♥ Chapter 5

"Amy!" Mills waves at me, beaming. "You decided to come. Hi, Clover." I hope Mills doesn't spill the beans.

Sophie looks at me suspiciously. "Why are you grinning like that, Amy?" she snaps. "You look mental."

Then her eyes linger on Clover as if she can't quite place her. Sophie likes to place people. She's very territorial.

"Who's she?" she asks Mills, staring at Clover openly. "How do you know her?" Like Clover, Sophie can also be appallingly direct.

Mills opens her mouth to say something, but Clover quickly cuts in: "I'm an old friend of Amy's. From way back."

Mills throws me a look, and I touch my finger to my lips. She shrugs and stays quiet.

Clover says, "And who are *you*?" She looks Sophie up and down, taking in her Ugg boots, ironed and back-combed hair that stinks of almond-sweet hairspray, dark eyeliner, and striped tank top. Sophie's baby-pink bra straps are showing, and the cups are pinching her breasts. I wonder if Clover's noticed. Clover has a thing about badly fitting underwear.

"Sophie. Amy's *best* friend." Her voice is as prickly as a rosebush.

Clover's having none of it. "Great," she says smoothly. "Then, you'll let us cut the queue." She turns to the boys directly behind Mills and Sophie. "I'm sure you won't mind, lads. We're just joining our friends."

"No problemo, girls." A pimply red-haired guy with a thin, weasel-like face gives us a gappy smile. "Be my guest." He waves a hand in front of him. As we squeeze in beside Sophie and Mills, I feel a sharp tweak on my bum and swing around.

"Did you just pinch me?" I demand, outraged.

He winks at me cheekily. "What if I did?"

Clover squares up her shoulders. She may be small — smaller than me, in fact, and I'm only five foot — but she has presence. She pokes his pigeon chest with a finger. "Have some respect. What are you, *two*? Only toddlers pinch." She reaches up and grabs the top of one of his ears — which is fleshy and looks like a pink bat's wing — between her thumb and forefinger. "See how you like this." She pulls down.

He squeals. "*Ow!* Let me go, ya crazy cow."

"What's going on here?" A beefy bouncer in a tight T-shirt and shiny black trousers marches over. He looks like a mountain gorilla, stooped, with extra-long arms and huge paddle-size hands. You wouldn't mess with him.

"This little rat pinched my friend's bum," Clover tells him, batting her eyelashes.

The bouncer looks the boy up and down. "Did he, now? Do you think young ladies like that kind of thing, Sonny Jim?" He hitches his thumb toward the road. "Right, off with you, pal. Yer barred."

"But they cut the queue," the boy protests.

"I don't care. Just get." The bouncer moves his thumb again.

Clover gives the bouncer a winning smile and touches his forearm gently with her hand, her fingers lingering on his freckled skin. "Thank you so much."

He blushes, clearly smitten. "Yer welcome. Sorry about that, ladies. Come with me." We follow him to the front of the queue, and then he waves us inside.

"No charge for these girls," he tells the woman at the door. "They've just been sexually harassed."

Once inside, Sophie looks at Clover with new respect. "That was cool. Can I get you a drink?" she asks, fishing in her silver shoulder bag for her wallet.

Clover says, "Absolutely." She's not one to turn down a freebie.

We get drinks and then position ourselves against a wall, watching the action.

The rugby club smells sweet and musky, a mixture of smuggled-in Bacardi Breezers, sweat, and hormones. The floor is sticky from spilled drinks, and the DJ loves his bass; my stomach is vibrating with every thud. I spy a few emo kids from school, huddled in a corner, including the two Pippi Longstocking girls. One of them is nibbling at the skin around her thumb; the other is staring at the floor. Cheery little souls.

"Hey, girls," Mills says. "What do you think?" She nods at Brett, who is throwing shapes around the dance floor to a remixed version of "Umbrella." "He's cute."

"He looks full of himself." Sophie sniffs. "And he's about sixteen. Way out of your league, Mills."

"You think?" Clover says. There's a dangerous twinkle in her eye.

Sophie looks at her. "Boys like that don't go out with normal girls. They go for D4s with modeling contracts."

Clover just smiles at her a little smugly and gives a soft "huh." We exchange a look. We know better. Wendy. She's no D4 model.

"What?" Sophie puts her hands on her hips.

Clover says, "Boys like that *deserve* D4 models. They're not good enough for anyone else. They deserve brain-dead bimbos."

Sophie's lower lip drops, and her mouth gapes open like a goldfish. Talking to a wannabe D4, Clover has pushed the wrong button.

"D4s have brains," Sophie snaps. "They have everything. Brains, looks, cool clothes. The best-looking boyfriends. You don't know what you're talking about. You're just jealous because he"— she points at Brett —"wouldn't go near someone like *you*."

Clover's back stiffens. "Is that right?"

"Yeah," Sophie says firmly. "It is."

Clover watches Brett for a moment. I have to admit: for a pig, he can dance. Then her gaze shifts to one of his friends, an olive-skinned boy with shoulder-length surfer hair who's all puppet arms and legs on the dance floor, but he's so good-looking, it doesn't really matter.

Without taking her eyes off him, Clover hands me her drink. She leans in. "Watch and learn, Beanie."

"I bet she can't even dance," Sophie says snidely as Clover walks away from us.

Mills stares at Sophie. "Get over yourself."

Sophie throws Mills a daggers look, and Mills cringes.

I ignore their bickering and glue my eyes to Clover's back. Because *I've* seen Clover dance. And my little bubble of excitement has just become the size of a hot-air balloon.

♥ Chapter 6

"Oh, my God," Sophie says. She's so shocked she's forgotten to pronounce it "Eoi, moi Gawd," the D4 way (it's their fave expression). Mills makes a squeaking noise, like a strangled mouse.

I just grin from ear to ear.

Clover's on fire. She's snaking her body like a professional. Her pale blond hair is flying around her head, lit up by the multicolored lights like a moving halo. She shimmies her hips and rakes her shoulders backward and forward to the music.

Clover loves dancing. When she was younger, she used to spend hours in her bedroom every night, wheeling and spinning until she was dizzy. One night she jumped off the bed (practicing a star jump) and landed awkwardly. Gramps was in the living room below at the time, and he thought there'd been an earthquake. Clover's ankle was so badly sprained he had to bring her to the emergency room. They bandaged it up and gave her crutches. She couldn't walk properly for weeks. It's a shame she's tone-deaf 'cause she would have been brilliant in *Grease* or *Mamma Mia!*

Even Brett is staring at Clover. Mainly at her legs. She's crouching down now and pumping her arms to the beat, every muscle in her calves and thighs tight as she balances in a low squat. Then she jumps up and dirty-dances up and down the dark-haired boy's body, a wicked grin on her face. After the initial shock, he gets really into it, pressing his body against hers, his hands holding her waist. They look amazing together. Brett's eyes are stuck to them like Velcro.

Mills nudges me in the side. "I'd love to be able to dance like that."

"She's probably had classes." Sophie sniffs.

"You're just jealous," I say, "because Clover's so cool."

"Yeah, whatever," Sophie snaps.

I smile to myself. Clover is getting under Sophie's skin. Excellent.

As I watch, Brett starts to dance right beside Clover

and the surfer. Eventually Brett grabs his friend's shoulder and says something to him. The dark-haired boy stops dancing, excuses himself to Clover, and walks toward the bar.

Clover and Brett stare at each other, their faces only inches apart. Clover's face is shiny from dancing, and her chest is heaving. She licks her upper lip with the point of her tongue, and Brett's mouth falls open. Clover begins to dance again, slowly at first. He joins her, and they look incredible together. The floor clears around them as everyone watches. I've never seen anything like it — it's like something out of *Step Up* or a raunchy version of *High School Musical*.

"Did you see that, Sophie?" I ask her. I can't help myself.

Sophie says nothing for a moment. Then she surprises me. "OK, I was wrong. He likes her. Big deal."

Clover spins around, and as she's facing us, she rolls her eyes dramatically. I laugh. Clover glances at her watch, then turns and grabs Brett around the neck. Seconds later they're kissing.

"Look! Look!" Mills squeals, jumping up and down with excitement.

Sophie is pretending to be unimpressed. But she's watching pretty carefully for someone who's not interested. Probably taking mental notes. I know for a fact she's only kissed one boy, and that was only for a few seconds.

Brett is really going for it. He's holding the back of Clover's head, and his arms are octopussing up and down her back.

Seconds later Clover pulls away and shrieks, "Eoi, moi Gawd! Eoi, moi Gawd! Eoi, moi Gawd!" in a cut-glass D4 accent. Her hands are flapping around in the air like bird's wings, and then I spot it. Huge glossy red dollops on her white T-shirt. They're dripping from her mouth.

The whole hall stops, and everything seems to go into slow motion, like it's happening underwater. The only sound is the *thump*, *thump*, *thump* of the music.

"That's blood!" Sophie shrieks. She points at Brett. "He bit her. That boy bit her."

Sophie loves being the center of attention. You can always rely on her to make a scene. She rushes over to Clover, takes her hand, and drags her toward the girls' loo.

"Eoi, moi Gawd!" Sophie shouts loudly, so that everyone can hear her. "You poor thing. You must be utterly traumatized."

"Oh, I am, I am," Clover says. I can tell she's trying not to laugh. She secretly hands me something. I clutch it in my palm until we get into the loos. Then I look down. Two empty plastic vials in the shape of large pills. Fake blood from the joke shop. Now I understand. I feel a little sorry for Brett — it is rather extreme. But I can't help smiling to myself all the same.

While Clover washes the "blood" off her face and dabs at her T-shirt with a piece of damp, crumbling toilet paper, Sophie tells the audience in the loo about Clover's horrific experience. The D4s are all ears, especially a certain girl named Charlene.

♥ Chapter 7

I race over to Clover's after school on Monday. She's lying sideways on Gran's old beach lounger, face buried in the flowery orange-and-green 1970s material of the cushion. She's snoring loudly, making a strange clucking noise at the back of her throat, her breath whistling in and out of her mouth. Mum says Clover's always snored, even as a baby, but Clover denies it.

She looks really cute, and I take a picture of her with my mobile. Hearing the click, she stirs, flops onto her back, and, putting her hand over her eyes to shade them from the bright sunlight, gives me a lazy-cat smile.

"Hey, Beanie." She rolls up her tank top and tucks it into the bottom of her bra, exposing her flat stomach to the rays. "Isn't this sun gorge? How was school?"

I sit down on the edge of the lounger, almost toppling it. I pull over a sun-bleached green plastic chair instead. "OK. Did you hear from Wendy? I'm dying to know."

Clover grins. "Sure did. The plan worked."

"Really?"

"Yep. Her e-mail's probably still up on the screen if you want to have a look. Big success. And Saffy likes my piece on revenge. She said it's very original, if a little dark. She's edited it down, something about libel laws and getting sued."

"How exciting! Your first article. Can I read it?"

Clover grins. "Sure." She reaches down, grabs a purple plastic folder off the grass, and hands it to me. I start to read an extract.

Wronged by a Boy? Want Revenge?
Read Our Fab Revenge Tips from the *Goss*'s
Resident Revenge Expert, Clover M. Wildgust

"Expert?" I look at Clover and raise my eyebrows.

Clover laughs. "Hey, I dealt with Brett, didn't I?"

I smile and read on.

Girls, you need to plan your revenge carefully. Think of it as a military campaign. Decide if you want to attack the enemy or defend yourself and your good name.

Attack Ideas

✱ Plant a pink Harlequin romance novel in his school bag. When he pulls his books out, he'll get quite a shock. Hopefully his classmates will see it too!

✱ If you know where he keeps his mobile phone, set the ringtone to play a piece of warbling opera singing or classical music. The louder, the better.

✱ Plant pink sticky notes on his books and in his lunch box: *I love you, darling. XXX Mummy; Remember how special you are, Pooky. XXX Mumsie; Love is a great big hug from Mummy. XXX.* They'll go down like a treat.

✱ Tell the biggest gossip in your class that he secretly does ballet classes and plays with LEGO.

And if you want to get really nasty:

✱ Smear the inside of his school bag with mackerel pâté, or pop a mackerel sandwich in one of the pockets (boys never clean out their bags). Girls, after a few days, it'll yang like nothing human!

✱ Plant mustard and watercress seeds at the back of his locker — and add water, of course! Boys never clean out their lockers, either: it'll be a lush green forest before he even notices.

Defense Ideas

Remember, the best revenge of all is success. Yours!

✱ Write a short story or a poem and get it published.

✱ Write a song and sing it at a school concert.

✱ Join the drama society and bag the leading role (or the leading man!).

Get on with your life and enjoy yourself, and you'll soon forget all about him — I promise!

I'm impressed. "Where did you get the idea for the sticky notes, Clover? That's inspired."

"My warped mind does come in useful sometimes," she says with a grin. "And a guy in the office called Brains came up with the Harlequin one. His mum reads them. She put one in his school bag once by mistake; it got mixed up with his own books. He's never forgotten it."

"What does Brains do? Is he a journalist?"

"Nah. He's supposed to be the designer and IT guy, but he spends most of the time surfing weird sites and singing to himself. He sits beside me when I'm in the office." Clover works from the *Goss* office two days a week; the other days she works from home.

"It's brilliant! But mustard and watercress and mackerel?" I say, wrinkling my nose. "Gross! Isn't that a bit extreme?"

"Don't get all pious on me. I took all the really bad suggestions out. Saffy took exception to the one about sending dead floral wreaths, or letters from Sheep Lovers Anonymous, or anything to do with ex-boyfriend voodoo dolls.

"Anyway, I'm glad you like it, and thanks for all

your help on Friday night. I'm taking a well-deserved break now. I was up all night finishing my agony aunt page and the revenge article, and I'm bushed." She leans back against the beach lounger again and closes her eyes. "Go into my office and read Wendy's e-mail while I catch some rays."

I sit down at Clover's desk and open her laptop. Her office smells of the spray-on sunscreen she uses. Vanilla. *Dear Clover,* I read on the laptop screen.

Thank you, thank you, thank you. That was you with Brett, wasn't it? On Friday at the Sinister Nite? It must have been you.

As soon as I walked into school today, this girl, Charlene, came up to me—and Charlene never talks to me—and said, "Did you hear the goss? Brett Stokes bit this girl on Friday night when they were snogging. Took a huge chunk out of her. There was blood everywhere. Didn't you used to go out with him? Are you OK? No wonder you broke it off."

Isn't that incredible? It's all over school. Brett isn't in today, but the D4s are already calling him Bram, you know, after the guy who wrote *Dracula,* Bram Stoker.

Clover, thanks SO MUCH for your help. I'm

going to tell all my friends about you. I bet you'll
get loads of letters after this.
    Your fan forever,
    Wendy

I sit back in the swivel chair and smile to myself.
I'm so pleased it's all worked out for Wendy. I hate to
say it, but Clover's right: maybe sometimes you do
have to take action. Life moves pretty quickly, and
if you're not careful, it can whiz right by you while
you're waiting for something exciting to happen.

Spurred on by Clover's success, I flex my fingers,
quickly click onto my Bebo page, and start to update
it before I change my mind. I'm tired of being anonymous. It's time to take a leap of faith, to be myself,
and see what happens. What have I got to lose?

♥ Chapter 8

On Wednesday I'm on the train on the way home from school when Clover rings me on my mobile. She's in a complete state yet again. She's been overwhelmed by e-mails since the Frite Nite success — Wendy is obviously spreading the word — and she needs my help.

"Hey, Beanie, what am I supposed to tell a girl whose sister has nicked her boyfriend?" I can hear the shuffling of paper in the background. "And how should I know the true identity of the *Mona Lisa? Hello?*"

"Lisa Gherardini," I murmur. It was in the news recently, and we'd talked about it in history only last week.

"See, you're so much smarter than I am. Help!"

Another shuffling sound. "And I have one here about someone who's in love with her art teacher. Yuck!" From the tightness of her voice, I can tell she's about to explode.

"Hang in there, Clover," I say. "I'll be over as soon as I can."

I stare out the window and think about my own art teacher, Mr. Olen, or Mark, as he likes us to call him. Mid-twenties, chocolate-brown eyes, closely cropped dark hair, slim and muscular from marathon running. He'd actually be quite fanciable if he didn't already love himself so much. He says he's only teaching art until his own work is discovered, not that the galleries appreciate him, as he's always telling us. Did you know that galleries take up to 50 percent when they sell an artist's painting? Sometimes more. Mark has very strong feelings on the subject.

Seth, who sits beside me in art, says Mark has a chip on his shoulder the size of a redwood tree and should do less complaining and more painting. Seth's quiet. He mostly keeps himself to himself when he's not going on about trees (he has a thing about them) and how abstract art rules. Sophie and Mills think he's a complete weirdo.

He used to have a pet iguana named Rothko before he died (the iguana I mean, not Seth —

although Rothko the artist's dead too). Seth carved a special wooden headstone for him in art class. But at least he's not a brain-dead Crombie. And he does have great taste in art. And cool hair, dark blond and floppy.

When I get home, I walk into the kitchen to ask Mum if I can run over to Clover's. But Mum's upstairs having a nap and Dave's holding down the fort, so I have to ask him instead.

"I'm afraid it's a no, Amy," he says. "I'm sorry, but your mum needs help this evening. I'm working nights this week — you know that. You can go to Clover's tomorrow." He's standing at the sink, cradling a blue Yorkie mug in his two hands and watching Alex chase the neighbor's cat around the garden. Alex is screaming at the top of his lungs. Evie's asleep in her pram in the telly room. "You're always over there," he adds. "One night at home won't do you any harm."

I stick my tongue out at him when he isn't looking. "But she needs me today."

He throws the dregs of his coffee down the sink and then starts to wash out the mug under the tap, sticking his right hand into it and swirling his fingers about.

"She really needs me," I repeat, my arms folded over my chest. What there is of it.

"Clover?" He gives a laugh that comes out like a snort. "She doesn't need anyone."

"What do you mean?"

"Nothing." He puts the mug upside down on the draining board with a *clunk* and turns to look at me. "Look, your mum's really tired. Evie will be up soon, and Alex needs a bath."

I groan. "I'm not bathing him. He always soaks me."

"Amy, you're part of this family, and you have to pull your weight. And this Saturday —"

I interrupt him before he starts getting any more slave-labor ideas. "I'm going to Dad's. For the whole weekend." I smile at him smugly.

That stops him in his tracks. I haven't actually arranged anything, but Dad loves having me over. I'm not treated like some sort of Victorian servant at *his* house.

Dave's forehead wrinkles deeply, like a character out of *Star Trek*. "Are you sure? Sylvie didn't say anything about it. We're supposed to be going out for pizza and a movie, remember? Gramps said he'd babysit."

Oops, I'd forgotten all about Dave's movie trip, just the three of us, no babies. He's been trying to organize it for weeks. I think quickly. "It must have slipped Mum's mind—you know what she's like at the moment. She's Zombie Mom. We can do it some other time."

He rubs his stubbly neck with his hands. He has really dark stubble that grows very quickly. If he doesn't shave at least once a day, he looks like a pirate or one of the Sopranos. "You're right, I guess," he says. "Are you staying over at your dad's?"

"Yes, if it's OK, I'd really like to go. I need to talk to him about something."

He looks at me, a strange expression I can't quite read on his face. "About what?"

"Just things." I'm lying. I don't really need to talk to Dad at all. It just came out.

Then he nods. "Fine," he says, sounding a little cross. "If it's that urgent, I'll drop you off on Saturday afternoon. I'm sure Art can bring you home on Sunday. As long as he doesn't have an important golf match or something."

"Thanks," I say grudgingly. I only agree because Dad lives in Castleknock, which is miles away. It takes two bus rides to get there. I'll take my iPod so I won't have to talk to Dave in the car.

"It's a date." He winks at me.

Eeeuw. I just ignore him and walk out of the kitchen. He's such a nerd.

I run upstairs to ring Dad on my mobile from my bedroom. If Dave says something to Mum and she gets to Dad first, I won't be popular. I don't need any more grief than I'm already getting.

"How's my favorite daughter?" Dad says. He sounds very cheerful. I can hear a whirring noise in the background.

"Your *only* daughter," I point out. "Where are you?"

"In the back garden. Cutting the grass. You know what Shelly's like. Complete slave driver." He gives a rattling laugh that turns into a cough. Dad gave up smoking recently after twenty years, and his chest is still a bit funny from it. The cutting-the-grass thing is a first; Dad never used to cut the grass when he lived here. Mum was always complaining about it.

I don't like Dad's girlfriend, Shelly. In fact, I rarely acknowledge her at all if I can help it. And I've never uttered her name, not once. It requires quite a lot of effort to remember to say "she" or "her" all the time, but it's worth it. Mum doesn't use her name either; she calls her "Little Miss Perky" or "the Secretary."

Today I need to keep Dad on my side, so I laugh too. "Hey, can I stay over on Saturday?" I say, coming straight to the point. I hear a dog yapping, and Dad turns off the lawn mower.

"That's better," he says. "I can hear you now. The puppy hates the mower. What did you say about Saturday?"

"What puppy?" I say, my voice a little sharper than I intend.

There's silence for a moment, then a sharp yelping followed by Dad saying, "Down, Justin, there's a good boy. Can you take him, Shelly? I'm on the phone with Amy. Sorry about that, Amy love. We only got him yesterday, and he's a bit unsettled."

I feel like someone's just poured concrete into my stomach and is stirring it around with a great big stick. *He promised*, I think, my eyes starting to smart.

He continues, "I know you wanted to be with us when we went to the animal shelter, but Shelly thought—"

"Listen, I have to go. See you Saturday. Dave will drop me off in the afternoon. After lunch. Is that OK?"

"Great. You're not upset, are you? I'm sorry if you're disappointed about the puppy, only—"

"Bye, Dad." I click off my mobile and drop back against my bed. Tears spill from my eyes and wet the pillow beneath me. Why did Shelly have to go and spoil things yet again? Everything was fine until she came along.

"Amy?" Mum knocks on my bedroom door. "Can I come in?"

"No! I'm getting changed." I hear her walk away. I lie very still as streams of hot, angry tears roll down my cheeks.

There's a rap on my bedroom door. I look at my watch. It's just after eight, and apart from the nightmare that was Alex's bath, and then dinner, I've been up here all evening. Alex created a tidal wave by shifting his tubby pink bum from one end of the bath to the other, soaking the bathroom floor. Water dripped through the gap between the side of the bath and the linoleum, down through the ceiling, and onto the hall floor. Of course I got blamed for not keeping a proper eye on him. I tried to explain that I was too busy wiping the soapy water out of my eyes as he kept splashing me, but Mum was having none of it.

"Ah, Amy," she said. "He's only a toddler. You could have brought the whole ceiling down." He may be small, but he's pure evil sometimes, and he knows exactly what he's doing. He has Mum wrapped around his pudgy little finger.

Clover bounds in the door without waiting for an answer to her knock, like Tigger after too much sugar.

"Oi, Beanie, what's up? I was worried; you never rang me back. And Sylvie says you're in a stinker." She sits on the side of my bed and lies back, her head pressing into my stomach.

I sit up and push her head away. "Get off," I say. "You're heavy."

"Must be all the brains in there." She smiles at me. She has pink lip gloss on her slightly gappy front teeth. "You look terrible. What's wrong? Boy trouble?" She tilts her head. "Go on, you can tell me."

I shake my head but say nothing.

"Beans. It's me, your fave person in the whole world." She scrunches up her nose, which makes her look like a rabbit. "Go on, tell me. It can't be that bad. I brought some new letters to show you. You think your life is doggy doo — wait till you read these. Bound to cheer you up. You can help me answer them. But back to you first; what's up, jelly tot?"

"It's *her*, OK? Not a boy." I'm dying to tell someone. Mills isn't answering her mobile, and Sophie would probably just laugh at me. I hope Clover will understand. "Little Miss Perky's only gone and ruined everything again."

Clover makes a face. She doesn't like Shelly, either. "Go on," she says.

"They've got a new puppy. Justin."

"Justin?" Clover snorts. "What's wrong with Rover or Shep?"

"I know, I know. She has this sad thing for Justin Timberlake. Anyway, Dad promised I could go to the animal shelter with him. Help choose a new puppy. And name him or her. We hadn't decided on the sex. But they went yesterday, without me. It was her idea. She didn't want me there." I made the last bit up, of course, but I'm sure it's true.

"I'm not surprised you're upset," Clover says. "What a witch! But she's such a control freak. Wait till the puppy poops all over her precious lawn and digs up her flower beds. And eats all the gold tassels on the end of her curtains. She'll probably beg you to take him away then."

"Dave has allergies," I remind her. "We can't have any pets."

"Sorry, I forgot. Bummer." She pushes my hair back off my face, her hand cool against my hot cheek. "Look, Beanie, your dad's with Shelly now, and you'll just have to accept that, even if she is a bit of a ditz. But I'm sorry about the puppy thing. Justin." She shakes her head. "Poor dog. What breed? Another Lab?"

When we were all living together — me, Mum, and Dad — we had a black Labrador named Timmy.

He died three days after Mum and Dad told me they were separating. Great timing.

"I never asked," I say.

Clover walks over to my chest of drawers and pokes around in my makeup bag. "What are you doing on Saturday morning?" She picks up my new Juicy Tube and tries it out.

"Nothing, why?"

"I'm taking you shopping, that's why." She puts the lip gloss back and smacks her lips together. "Mmm, watermelon, delish."

I manage a smile. Shopping with Clover is always fun.

"That's better," she says. "You have a lovely smile, Beans. You should use it more often."

"Clover! You sound just like Mum."

Clover frowns. "Can't be helped, I guess. We are sisters." She jumps onto the bed and throws her arms around me, hugging me tight.

"Get off, you mentaller." I laugh and swat her away as she pulls up my T-shirt and blows a sticky lip gloss raspberry on my stomach.

It's hard to be in a bad mood with Clover around.

♥ Chapter 9

By Saturday morning I can't wait to get out of the house. I put on some music while I'm packing my bag for Dad's place, and Evie starts crying.

"Turn that down, Amy!" Mum yells up the stairs. "I've just put the baby down for her nap." Then Evie really starts to bawl.

Dave stomps up the stairs, muttering, "Amy, have you no brain?"

I stick my head out of my room. "I didn't do it on purpose."

"I'll have to take her for a walk now." He rakes his hands through his hair. I feel a little sorry for him; he looks wrecked. There are two dark, cuplike hollows under his eyes, like he's been in a concentration camp.

We've been studying World War II in school, and it's shocking stuff. Miss Ireland, our history teacher, invited this old Jewish lady, Mrs. Harris, in to talk to us. Mrs. Harris hadn't been in a concentration camp herself — she'd managed to escape with her dad before she had been found. They'd traveled to London and then to Ireland. But she had lost a lot of her family in Auschwitz, a camp in Poland. She was so good at telling stories, she made it all come alive. She showed us slides of some of the camps and also a few old grainy black-and-white photographs of her mum and her sister, Rebecca, who had been killed in a camp. Makes you think.

"I thought you were on nights," I say to Dave.

"I am. But your mum needs help."

I feel bad. When he's on nights, he doesn't get home till seven a.m. It's now ten, so he's only had three hours' sleep, tops.

I sigh. "I'll take her for a walk. In fact, if Clover doesn't mind, we can probably take Evie shopping with us."

His eyes light up. "That'd be brilliant. Thanks, Amy." He steps toward me, arms out, like he wants to hug me, but I back away.

"Give me five minutes," I tell him.

* * *

As we walk down the road toward Dun Laoghaire town center, Clover insists on pushing the buggy. It's an old black-and-gray Mamas & Papas thing Dave found on eBay. It was secondhand when Alex had it, and it's even more battered now. I wanted them to get a red Bugaboo for Evie, like you see the cool mums and dads pushing down the pier, but Dave's really into recycling and said the old buggy was grand. Grand for him maybe. I think Mum was a bit disappointed — she likes the Bugaboos too — but she said Dave was right; it was a waste of money when we had a perfectly good one already.

"She's like a little doll," Clover says, smiling down at Evie.

"When she's not crying," I point out. "Let's hope she stays asleep, or we'll be thrown out of all the shops for noise pollution. She's like a fire alarm when she gets going."

Clover starts to look concerned.

I say, "Don't worry. She'll stay asleep as long as we keep moving."

Clover stops outside a small shop squeezed in beside a flower shop and Dunnes Stores. "Here we are," she announces with a wave of her hand. "Una's."

I stare in the pink-framed window. It doesn't look

very promising. There's a mannequin dressed in the kind of tentlike nightie a granny would wear: plain white brushed cotton with a pink ribbon threaded around the top like a necklace. Beside it is a fan of plain white Sloggi knickers and two matching sensible white lacy bras — the kind my mum usually wears — displayed on clear plastic headless frames. There's even a pair of striped blue-and-white woolly bed socks.

Clover laughs. "OK, so the window isn't very inspiring. But Una really knows her stuff." She nods at the door. "Can you get that for me?"

Before I have a chance, a tiny woman appears in front of us and whisks open the door. She's obviously stronger than she looks. She's wearing a cream roll-neck sweater and a tweedy brown skirt, and she has a tape measure hanging around her neck like a scarf. Her breasts are ample and round, like two Jell-O molds, and I try not to stare. They're pretty impressive.

"Hello, Clover," she says. "What a pleasure. And who's this young lady?" She smiles at me, and her primrose-blue eyes twinkle through her gold-rimmed glasses. She must be at least seventy.

"This is my niece Amy," says Clover. "And this is my other niece Evie." She points into the pram. Una has a quick look at Evie but doesn't seem all that interested, which is refreshing. Normally people go all gooey over Evie, especially old ladies.

"So what can I do for you today?" says Una. "I have some gorgeous new black Triumph push-up bras."

"I'm looking for something for Amy," says Clover. "Something to give her a bit of a shape."

I can feel my face go bright red, and I stare at Evie, who is starting to stir.

When I look up, Una is giving me a bright, friendly smile. "First, let's get you into the fitting room and see what size you are." She whips the measuring tape from her neck and walks briskly toward the chintz-curtained cubicle at the back of the store.

My heart sinks into my boots. "Does she have to measure me?" I whisper to Clover.

"She'll do it over your top," Clover says. "Don't worry, Beanie. You don't have to strip."

Evie starts to mew like a kitten, and Clover wheels the buggy backward and forward. She nudges me with her shoulder. "Go on."

Clover's right; it's fine. I put my arms out straight, making a T-shape, then Una measures me outside my top. It only takes a few seconds, and I hardly even feel the tape measure. "You're a 32A," she says confidently. "What age are you, dear?"

"Thirteen."

"A very common size for your age. And we have lots of lovely bras that'll fit you. Follow me."

"She's a 32A," Una tells Clover.

Clover nods. "Thought as much."

Una putters around the shop, picking out bras for me.

"Do you mind?" I hiss at Clover while Una's distracted. "Stop discussing my bra size."

Clover ruffles my hair. "You are funny, Beanie. I'm a 34B myself. Sometimes a C depending on the make of the bra. I started off as a 32AA. Even smaller than you."

"Really?" I ask, starting to feel a little better. "A" sounds so teeny. But "AA" is even smaller.

"Sure."

Una hands me five bras. "Try these on," she says. "See which ones you like best. We have matching briefs too. All kinds of styles."

Apart from once, when Una throws back the curtain and checks if she's got the sizing right by gently tugging at the sides and adjusting the straps a little, I'm left alone to try on the bras. The first one is a plain white padded one that doesn't look like much, but when it's on, it gives me a lovely curvy shape and is dead comfortable. I wince when I see the price tag: thirty euros.

The second is adorable and white with delicate pale-red flowery embroidery. It's not quite as comfortable as the first one, but it's the kind you'd be proud to show off in the locker room. Mills would love it; she's a real girlie-girl. The third and fourth are similar to the first: both plain white, one with padding, the other without. Nothing special. But the fifth takes my breath away. I'd never pick it out myself: sky-blue lace with subtle, dark pink embroidery along the scalloped edges. It's heavenly, a really special bra.

"How are you getting on, Beanie?" Clover says from outside the curtain. "Can I have a peek?"

I'm about to say "No!" when I change my mind. I stand up straight, push my shoulders back, and say, "All right." Clover pokes her head through the curtain and gives me a grin. "Looking good, Beanie. See, I told you a decent bra makes all the difference. Pick your fave three. And hurry up. Evie's starting to cry."

"Are you sure?"

"Yep. Saffy paid me extra for that revenge article. Besides, I owe you for all your help with the agony aunt page."

Three! I'm in bra heaven. Clover's the best.

Walking back home, I swing the flesh-pink Una's bag by my side. I chose the white one with the red flowers, the sky-blue lacy one, and the comfortable white one, and Clover insisted on buying the matching lacy boy shorts to go with the first two. She said no to the thong. She said Sylvie would have a fit. She's probably right. I'm not all that keen on thongs, anyway. They're so uncomfortable, and who wants to show off their naked bum cheeks? Apart from Sophie and the D4s, of course.

I haven't felt so good in a long time. "Thanks, Clover," I say as she hands Evie over at the front door. She has to meet Ryan in town for lunch and she's late, as usual. "You're the best."

"Hey, Beanie, can I ring you later? I still need advice on those letters."

"No problem. I'll be at Dad's; ring my mobile."

"Coola boola. See ya." She kisses her fingers and blows them at me as she dashes toward the gate.

♥ Chapter 10

It's way past eleven, but I can't sleep. My mind's hopping around like the Easter bunny. I'm lying in bed at Dad's, wondering what I've done to deserve such a cruddy life. I'm trying not to feel sorry for myself, but it's hard.

I'll rewind. We arrived at Dad's at four. We had to stop along the quays because Evie had filled the car with a horrible eggy stench, and Dave had to change her nappy on the backseat. Mum had needed a rest, so she stayed at home, and Dave had taken Alex and Evie in the car with us. Big mistake. Alex had cried for half an hour solid before I'd jammed a bottle of milk in his mouth and he'd finally fallen asleep. Evie'd slept for the first half an hour, and then she'd decided to stink out the car.

Her bum is red and raw from terrible nappy rash, so you have to change her instantly, or else her skin can get infected from the acidy poo. Sometimes I wish I didn't know so much about gross things like nappy rash. Sometimes I wish Mum hadn't had the babies. I know it's mean and selfish, but I can't help how I feel. They're so much work. But at least I'm free of all that at Dad's.

Or so I'd thought. You see, Dad had an announcement.

After I'd dumped my bag in my room, he brought me out to the back garden to meet Justin. Shelly was sitting on one of their *très* glam wooden garden chairs with its matching white padded cushion, like something from the poolside in an American movie, and she jumped up as soon as she saw me. She looked at Dad and gave him this funny look, and Dad shook his head a bit. I knew something was up. Then this puppy came flying over and jumped up, putting his little paws on my thighs. He was really cute, a springer spaniel, with lots of caramel-colored fluffy fur.

"We have something to tell you," Dad said, holding the back of one of the chairs. "Sit down, Amy."

He sounded all serious, so I sat down without a word. Shelly's hands were shaking for some reason, which was a bit odd; she wasn't usually the nervous type. She held Justin's collar with her hand and then pulled him onto her knee. But he was too skittish, so she let him down again, and he went tearing around the garden. She frowned and brushed off her white jeans. I was delighted to see he'd left muddy brown marks behind him. I looked up at Dad, and he had this strange expression on his face, kind of worried but happy. And then it came to me. They were getting married. I felt hollow.

But then Dad said, "We're having a baby, Amy. Shelly's pregnant. We wanted you to be the first to know. You're going to have another baby brother or sister."

"Half-brother or sister," I said, standing up. "Excuse me." I felt sick and I just wanted to get out of there. I could feel Shelly's eyes on me, and I didn't want to cry in front of her.

"Amy," Dad said, "where are you going?"

"To the loo. Is that a problem?"

As I walked inside, I could hear the puppy yapping and Shelly saying, "I knew she wouldn't be happy. I did warn you. But oh, no —"

Ten minutes later, Dad found me in my bedroom. By that stage I was debating whether to go home or not. He sat down on the bed and put his arms around me. I shrugged them away, and he backed off.

"Don't be like that," he said. "I know it's a bit of a shock, but I want you to be happy for us."

"I'm sorry," I said, tears filling my eyes. "I don't want to be like this, but I can't help it. I'm sick of babies."

Dad gave a laugh. "I know, love, but life goes on. Shelly's never had one of her own." He shrugged. "She's twenty-nine. It's time."

"She has years to go. Mum had Evie when she was thirty-seven."

"I know, but it wasn't her first. This is very special to Shelly."

"What about you? Do you want another baby?" I asked.

"Of course I do."

"Does this mean you'll be getting married?"

"Ah, there's something else I've been meaning to tell you."

And that was when he dropped his second bombshell of the day. Dad and Shelly had gotten married on their holiday in Barbados in March — without telling a soul. March! It is May. When had they been thinking of telling me, exactly?

When I've stopped crying, I ring Clover. I know it's late, but it's Saturday night; she's probably out somewhere exciting with her boyfriend, Ryan, having fun. But I feel so down, I need to talk to someone.

Clover answers her phone immediately. "Hey, Beanie, what's up?" I can hear music and laughter in the background.

"Where are you?"

"Ryan's place. I'll just pop outside; give me one sec. . . . Right, that's better. Shoot."

It all comes tumbling out. The whole story: the Barbados wedding, the baby, how confused I feel, how I want to die. As I'm telling her, tears run down my cheeks.

"You don't want to die, Beanie," she says calmly. "It's perfectly normal to feel a bit overwhelmed and upset. It's a lot to take in. What was your dad thinking? Listen, I'll come and collect you in the morning. We'll have lunch somewhere nice, and you can help me with the new agony aunt letters. That'll take your mind off it. Eleven, how does that sound?"

I wipe my tears away and give a hiccup. "That sounds perfect."

"And, Beanie?"

"Yes?"

"Love you, OK? That'll never change. Hang in there. See you in the morning."

♥ Chapter 11

Dad isn't thrilled that I'm dashing off with Clover before lunch, but as he's planned to play golf all afternoon, leaving me with the dreaded Shelly, he can't exactly complain. When Clover arrives at Dad's, she's not alone. Ryan, her latest beau, is sitting in the passenger seat: my seat! The Red Hot Chili Peppers are playing on the car stereo, and his head is bobbing backward and forward, his light brown hair rippling to the music. I stare at him for a second. Last time I saw him, he had tousled surfer hair; now he has a seventies indie-boy pudding bowl, shiny and sleek. With his slim face and cheeky grin, he just about carries it off. But it's close.

Clover opens the driver's door and pulls down her seat to let me into the back.

Ryan says, "Hiya, Amy. How's tricks?" and then goes back to his nodding-dog impression.

Clover catches my eye in the rearview mirror. She gives a little shrug with her eyebrows as if to say sorry. She's been pretty nice to me about Dad and everything, and I'm sure I'm wrecking her romantic Sunday morning, so I smile back at her.

"How's college?" I ask Ryan.

"Same old, same old," he says. "Exams coming up. I'll probably fail."

"No, you won't," Clover says. "Pay no attention to him, Beanie. He's been studying away every night. I've hardly seen him. I'm surprised he wanted to come out to play this morning. But he squeezed me in. Didn't you, babe?" Clover gives a laugh.

"Sure." Ryan flashes her a smile and then stares out the passenger window. I wonder if something's up. He's being a little odd, quiet. He's usually very chatty, cracking jokes and telling me about the new bands he's just discovered.

"So where are we off to?" I ask her.

She catches my eye. "The zoo. They have a new baby chimp and baby elephant. I've wanted to see them for ages, and seeing as we're so nearby. . . ." She trails off. "I know you're a bit old for the zoo, Green

Bean, but it'll be fun. I'll drop Ryan off in town first. He has to study."

I say nothing for a moment, and then I sit back in my seat and stare out the window. "OK," I say eventually. "The zoo it is." If Clover really wants to go, then I'll go. It's no big deal. And it's time I put my zoo demons to rest.

I was nine, nearly ten, the last time I went. Mum and Dad wanted to take me somewhere special for lunch, my choice; they had something to tell me. So I said I'd like to go to the zoo. I hadn't been for years, and it always reminded me of family days out, in the old days when Mum and Dad still smiled at each other occasionally.

So off we trooped, Mum and Dad in the front, me in the back, silent the whole way to Phoenix Park, home of Dublin Zoo. By the time we got there, it was gray and drizzling. I don't know what I'd expected: that Mum and Dad would miraculously start talking to each other just because we were surrounded by all these cool animals.

Well, it didn't happen. We had only gotten as far as the tigers before Dad's mobile rang. He walked off, saying he had to take the call. Mum stared after him, her eyes flat and dead.

"Great timing," she muttered. Then she said, "Whatever happens, remember how much we both love you, Amy." There were tears in her eyes.

I remember thinking that someone must be dying. Gramps maybe. Gran had died three months previously, and Gramps hadn't been the same since, according to Mum.

But it wasn't Gramps who was dying — it was their marriage. Later, we sat outside a fake African hut in the African Plains, eating burgers and chips and watching the little black-and-white-striped "train" that took you on a tour of all the African animals. It was really just rickety carriages pulled along by a glorified tractor. Not a train at all. Fake.

I listened as Mum told me how she and Dad didn't love each other anymore, that they had decided to live apart. I'd be living with her and spending every second weekend with Dad. As she spoke, I felt like I was on a cloud looking down at myself. The words went in, but I couldn't concentrate on their meaning. But I knew instantly that my life would never be the same again. Sophie's parents had divorced when she was five, and her mum is still bitter about it, even now.

Dad didn't say much. He just held the back of my chair as Mum spoke to me. I found out afterward that he'd been seeing Shelly for ages; they'd met in the bank. She was his secretary—what a cliché! But Mum said I wasn't to blame Shelly. They would have broken up, anyway; they hadn't been happy for a long time.

I knew it had nothing to do with me, but I still felt guilty. Maybe if I'd made a bigger effort to keep my room clean and gone to bed when Mum had asked me to, she wouldn't have been so tired all the time and Dad wouldn't have taken up with Shelly. But when I said this to Mum afterward, she just cried and said, "It has nothing to do with you, pet. It's just something that happens to grown-ups sometimes."

I grew up pretty quickly that year. So you can see why I wasn't exactly waving pom-poms like a cheerleader at Clover's choice of venue. But she couldn't have known; I'd never told her about it.

We're standing in the monkey house, Clover and I, when her mobile rings.

"I'll be back in a second, Beanie," she says, and walks outside.

Through the reinforced glass, I watch a baby chimp waddling around in his nappy. I know it's a "he" because there's a sign taped to the wall. WELCOME, BABY LIAM, BORN ON APRIL 12. He's so tiny that he trips over his own little feet, and I want to pick him up and give him a hug. He reminds me of Evie. I watch as his monkey mum strokes his head gently and gives him a little push. She turns her head and looks at me. Then she puts her leathery hand against the glass. It looks like one of Mum's muddy old gardening gloves.

I kneel down on the dusty concrete floor and put my own hand up to mirror it. She has a smushed-up, almost heart-shaped nose, and I stare into her eyes. The look she gives me is so human, so knowing, I gasp. I'm still reeling from that stare when Clover comes back. She's chewing on her lip and seems a little upset.

"What's up?" I ask.

"Ah, nothing." She crouches down beside me and puts her head on my shoulder. "So how are you holding up, Beanie?"

I shrug. I don't trust myself to talk without crying, so I say nothing.

"I'm sure you're hurting," she says. "But give it time. Once the baby is born, you'll be so excited that all this will be forgotten. I promise."

"You think?"

"Are you kidding?" She nudges me with her shoulder. "You know what you're like with teeny tinies.

You go gaga. You even love their smell. That's not normal."

She's right. I have this thing about sniffing babies' necks: they smell so fresh and innocent. Like a new cotton T-shirt. My gran used to do it too.

Our backs are pressed up against the glass. Most of the monkeys are outside, so there's no one in the monkey house except for us, Liam, and his mum.

"But I am sorry your dad hit you with all that news in one go," Clover says gently. "Talk about timing."

"Timing has never been Dad's thing." I tell her about Mum and Dad and what happened the last time I was at the zoo.

"*Siúcra*, Beanie," she says. "I'm so sorry, I had no idea. We could have gone somewhere else for lunch."

"And missed the monkeys?"

Liam's mum hits the glass behind us, and we both jump in fright. And then laugh.

"Let's get you home," Clover says, pushing herself to her feet and holding out her hand to pull me up.

"What about the baby elephant? And we may as well have something to eat now that we're here."

Her eyes sparkle. "Are you sure?"

I smile at her and nod. She's been so nice to me — it's the least I can do. She's a sucker for elephants;

she collects them. She has dozens of them on her windowsill, all joined by the trunk or the tail in long, flowing lines, like something out of *The Jungle Book*. She says they bring her good luck.

And, as she says, I'm a sucker for babies.

♥ Chapter 12

My ears are still ringing from lunch in the zoo's restaurant. The food was fine, but most of the tables were packed with screaming children. I get enough of that at home.

We decided to each grab an ice cream and scoot. Now we're sitting on a bench in front of the penguin enclosure. There's a faint smell of fish and musky animals, but it doesn't stop us from licking our ice cream — a white chocolate Magnum for Clover, who has a very sweet tooth; a strawberry-and-banana Solero for me.

"I hope you're not on a diet, Beanie," she said when I chose the Solero.

"I'd hardly be eating ice cream if I was," I pointed out.

"Frozen yogurt," she corrected me.

I smiled at her wanly. She can be so pedantic.

In fact, I am supposed to be on a diet — the NeanderThin diet — but I keep forgetting. It's supposed to make you lean, strong, and healthy, like a caveman. Honestly! I'm not making it up.

It was Sophie's idea. She thought we should all diet at the same time and support each other — diet buddies, she called it. Stupid idea if you ask me, but Mills is into it, so I play along for her sake. Janet Jackson lost fifty pounds on it apparently (according to Sophie, who got it from her mum's *Grazia* magazine). You have to eat fruit, nuts, vegetables, and steamed fish or chicken every three hours. Every three hours! It's hard to see how we'll lose weight if we keep eating so often, but Sophie says it's all based on metabolic science.

She has it all worked out. She gets her mum to make carrot, cucumber, and celery sticks for the three of us every day, each little packet wrapped in layers and layers of plastic wrap, like a caterpillar's chrysalis, which isn't very green of her. When I pointed this out, she just made a face at me and said, "I'll recycle it, *Amy*." When she said "Amy," she stretched her mouth downward and jutted out her chin. She looked just like a camel.

Clover and I lick our ice cream and watch the penguins fire themselves into the water like bullets, glide smoothly along the bottom of the slightly murky pool, and pop into the air again, like jack-in-the-boxes. It's very soothing.

It's funny how birds that swim so elegantly look so clumsy on land, waddling around like those plastic windup toys that move one foot in front of the other for a few seconds before falling down. Like Alex when he was just starting to walk.

"OK, Beanie?" Clover licks the stubby wooden Magnum stick and nips all the last shreds of chocolate off with her teeth. When it comes to ice cream and chocolate, she's always very thorough.

I nod.

"Let's get to work." She pulls out a green plastic document folder and shuffles through the pages. She seems to be looking for something. She pulls out a sheet and stuffs it back in her bag.

"What was that?" I ask.

"Nothing." She seems a little embarrassed.

"You're hiding something from me." I hold out my hand. "We're supposed to be a team. Hand it over."

She waits for a moment and then gives me a gentle smile. "You don't need to read that one, trust me, Beanie. Please?"

"I want to read them all," I say stubbornly.

She sighs, reaches back into her bag, and passes me the crumpled sheet. "There are seventeen letters, Beanie. We don't have to answer this one. There are plenty of other problems to deal with."

I read the letter and then I flick through the other sixteen. Clover's right — there are plenty of other problems, easy problems. How to tell your mum you need a bra; how to deal with zits on your chest and back; how to say no to a boy without losing him; how to deal with exam stress; but the one I want to answer is the first one. Because I know I can help.

To: agonyaunt@gossmagazine.com
Friday

Dear Clover,

My mum and dad separated eight months ago. I knew something was up — they were always arguing and shouting at each other, but I still can't believe it. I keep going over and over everything. Did I do something wrong? Did I cause them too much stress? Mum says I can be very moody sometimes.

The worst thing is now Mum and I are moving

in with her new boyfriend. He's a butcher. His wife died a few years ago. He's nice enough, but he has two sons who are older than me and it's all so weird. What if they catch me in the shower or something?

I can't tell my friends how I feel; their parents are all so normal. I'm afraid they'll laugh at me. I feel like such a freak. And so alone. Can you help me?

Carrie, 12

In the car on the way home, I write my reply in Clover's lined journalist's notebook.

Dear Carrie,
I'm so sorry to hear about your situation. My own parents separated when I was nine, and they're divorced now. At the beginning it hurt like hell. Every morning I'd wake up and after a few seconds I'd remember, and everything would seem sad and horrible. Mum spent a lot of the time crying. I used to catch her at it in the kitchen. She'd try to cover it up, saying she was cutting

onions or there was a sad song on the radio. Dad moved into an apartment in the city center. Like you, I kept wondering, Was it something I'd done? Was it my fault? But it really wasn't. I see that now. They just couldn't get along.

I'm telling you about my parents because you said you feel so alone. But I know for a fact that there are girls all over Ireland going through exactly the same thing. And it's tough. But I have to tell you — it does get better. My mum and dad are both much happier now, and they both have new partners.

I leave out the bit about the babies and the wedding. Oh, and Dave being a pain, and Shelly being a nightmare — that's too personal. Besides, I don't think it'd be all that helpful.

It's much better to have parents who are happy, even if it means that they have to live apart. I know it's hard, but it's important to remember that they both still love you and that none of it is your fault.

Try to get along with your stepbrothers.

I know it won't be easy, but I'm sure they'll find sharing their dad and their house with you and your mum hard too. You never know — down the line you might even be friends. At the very least, they might have cute mates! And don't worry about things too much — just be yourself and keep the bathroom door locked. Ask them to knock before they come into your bedroom, and say you'll do the same. If you all respect each other's privacy, it should be OK.

If you're feeling really bad about all of this, try talking to someone, an aunt maybe or a teacher, someone who will listen. It makes everything seem a little brighter.

And finally remember that even though things are difficult for you at the moment, it will all get easier. Hang in there, and remember you have friends and family who love you. I hope this helps.

All the best,
Clover X X X

When we pull up outside my house, I pass the notebook to Clover.

"Do you think it's all right?" I ask her nervously.

She reads it through and then says, "Hey, Beanie, when did you get so grown-up? Can I print it in the magazine?"

"You really want to print it?"

"Sure, it's perfect. And I think I'll write an article about dealing with new stepparents. What about 'Step Up' for a title? You're great at titles — got anything better?"

I stare out the windshield, lost in thought. A dog is peeing against a car's tire while his owner looks away and whistles.

Clover says, "I'm so sorry, Beanie. That was insensitive of me. I shouldn't be using your life to fill mag pages. I'm a bad person. But it's what journalists do, Beans. They mine their own lives for stories. I won't do the article, OK?"

"It's not that. I don't mind about the article." I pause for a second. "Clover. Be honest: do you think I'm overreacting?"

"To what?"

I shrug. "Dad and *her*. Getting married. The baby."

She gives a breathy snort. "Hello? No way! It's all pretty serious stuff. They definitely should have told you about getting married. You're part of their family."

"Not their new family."

Clover puts her arm around my shoulders. "Beans, things move on. Just because your dad is having a sproglet doesn't mean he doesn't love you. Maybe it'll make things easier between you and Shelly. She won't have a clue. She can't even light a fire or take the rubbish out without your dad's help. She's hopeless. A baby's going to completely floor her."

I smile. Clover's right. Shelly is pretty hopeless when it comes to practical things. "She'll get baby poo under her expensive false nails," I say. "She won't like that at all."

"And it'll puke all over her cashmere sweaters. She'll be in and out of the dry cleaner's like a yo-yo. She'll so need your help, Beanie. They both will."

"I suppose," I say grudgingly.

She gives me a squeeze. "You know what would really get up Shelly's perky little nose?"

"What?"

"Embrace this whole baby thing. Tell your dad how excited you are. That way she'll have nothing to complain about. She's probably sitting at home right now telling him how spoiled you are and how you're just jealous. Be the bigger person, Beanie."

I think about this for a second. "Pretend to be pleased for them? Even though I'm not?"

"You got it."

A car pulls up just behind us. A very familiar car. My palms start to feel a little sweaty. He must be here to talk to Mum, to tell her his news before I do.

"Clover, will you come in with me? That's Dad's car. Don't leave me on my own."

She turns around and stares into his convertible Mercedes, squinting her eyes a little. "At least he's left his secretary at home." She means Shelly. I smile a little.

"Hey, Art," Clover says brightly to my dad, stepping out of her Mini. "I'm just popping inside to say hi to Sylvie. See you in a mo'. Oh, and Amy has something to say to you."

"Clover!" I hiss at her, but she's at the front door by the time I climb out of the car.

Dad looks at me expectantly. I gulp and take a deep breath.

"I'm sorry," I say. "About yesterday. And about dashing off this morning. I just got a bit of a shock. Now that I've had time to think about it, I'm thrilled about the baby—really I am. Congratulations." I throw my arms around him and give him a tight hug. He smells like a pine forest: it's the expensive Italian aftershave he started wearing a few years ago. Mum hates it. "Eau de Loo Cleaner," she calls it.

"I'm so relieved," he says into my hair. "And I'm sorry too. For not telling you about the wedding. But Shelly —"

Something occurs to me, and I pull away. "Does Mum know about the wedding?"

He shakes his head. Is it my imagination, or does he suddenly look pale?

Jeepers, I think, *I wonder if Clover's —*

"ART GREEN!" Mum is standing at the front door, her hands on her hips. She has a scowl on her face that would frighten a grizzly bear.

Clover is standing behind her, and she looks at Dad and draws a finger slowly across her throat. I put my hand over my mouth to hide a nervous giggle. Dad is so dead.

His face drops. "Too late," he mutters, walking toward the house.

"What the hell do you think you're playing at?" Mum screams as soon as he's in the hall. I walk in after him. She slams the door behind us. Her face looks like thunder.

Clover grabs my arms and pulls me up the stairs. "You'd better stay out of the way, Beanie."

"But —" I begin.

"Please," Clover says, a serious look on her face. "Let me deal with this, all right?"

I nod and step into my room, but as soon as she's gone back downstairs, I creep down the hall so I can hear what's going on. Mum and Dad are in the kitchen now, but they're shouting, so I can still hear them.

"Have you no respect?" Mum's on a roll. "When were you going to tell me about the baby? At the christening? And I can't believe you got married without telling me."

I wince. Ah, so Mum knows everything. *Quick work, Clover.*

"Sylvie, just calm down for a second," Dad says.

"Calm down?" Mum shrieks. "Calm down? Are you *serious*?"

"God, you're impossible," he says. "I don't know how Dave puts up with it."

"Can I just say something here?" Clover interrupts.

"No!" Mum yells.

Dad says, "Let her speak, Sylvie."

"Look," Clover says. "Amy's upstairs and she can probably hear every word. Will you please stop shouting at each other? I know you've had a shock, Sylvie, and I'm sorry I told you like that, out of the blue. I only did it for Amy's sake, so you could help her through it. Not so you could rip chunks out of Art in front of her. The pair of you should grow up. You can't behave like this in front of Amy. You'll damage her for life.

"Now, I'm going home, and I'm taking her with me. After we've gone, you can fight all you like. But you know something? It's not fair. She's had a hard enough time of it already. Can't you both just get over your differences and learn to get along? For her sake?"

Silence. Then Mum starts to sob. "I'm so sorry. But it's not me — it's *him*. He's the one who went and married his dolly bird in secret."

"Just don't, Sylvie," Dad says. "I know you're jealous —"

"Jealous? Yeah, right, Art. I'm just dying to run off to some stupid tourist resort and get married in a straw hula-hula skirt."

"Enough!" Clover says. "I give up." I hear her march out of the kitchen. I close my door just before she whips it open.

"We're getting out of here," she says. "I'm sorry, Amy. They're acting like children. I don't know what to say."

"Mum's upset." I feel like I have to defend her. After all, it's Dad who's in the wrong.

Mum and Dad are standing in the hall as I follow Clover down the stairs.

"Sorry, Amy," Dad mumbles. He looks very sheepish. "I should have told you and Sylvie about the wedding weeks ago. I was too scared, to be honest. Shelly said—"

"Can't you forget about Little Miss Perky for just one minute?" Mum says. Then she cackles like a *Macbeth* witch. "Clearly not. After all, she's having your baby now, isn't she?"

"Mum." I'm appalled. I know she's upset, but that's not fair. She has two children with Dave, after all. And they're not even married.

"Sorry, Amy." Mum puts her hands to her face. "It's just a lot to take in."

The front door swings open, and Dave peers inside. "Oh, hi, everyone." Alex is asleep in the buggy on the path behind him. "Why the long faces?" he asks.

"Art and Shelly are married, and they're having a baby," Mum says.

Dave looks at Dad and smiles softly. "Congratulations, mate. I'm happy for you. When's it due?"

Things are so simple for Dave. Black and white. I wonder about him sometimes.

"September," Dad says.

Mum makes a funny little noise in the back of her throat, and her face crumples.

Dave looks at Mum. "Life moves on, Sylvie," he says gently.

Mum's eyes well up, and she turns on her heels and runs into the kitchen.

"Go easy on her, Art," Dave tells Dad. "She's a bit fragile at the moment. Evie's being difficult."

Dad nods and holds out his hand. "Thanks," he says.

Dave shakes it a little stiffly. "Best go now," Dave tells him firmly.

Dad murmurs, "Yeah," and walks out of the house.

Clover blows out her breath. "Jeepers, that was a bit intense. Where's Evie?"

"Upstairs having a nap," Dave says.

Clover smiles. "She's got my genes. She'll sleep through anything."

"Snores too," I add. "Just like you."

Clover makes a miffed horsey *humph* noise. "I do not snore, Beanie." She thumps me on the shoulder.

♥ Chapter 13

Later that afternoon, I go for a walk on Killiney Beach. Clover's snoozing on the sofa in her office, and Gramps is busy in the garden. Much as I'd love to help him deadhead the roses, I decide I need some time to think. I can't get Mum out of my head, her face mushed up with sadness. Does she still love Dad? Is that it? But what about Dave?

I walk over the old iron pedestrian bridge beside the train station, sand shuffling under my runners. As soon as I see the water, I start to feel a little better. I'm wearing the Gucci sunglasses with the rose-colored lenses that Clover gave me, and they're turning everything pink. The sea is magenta; the sky is lilac; the sand is the color of candyfloss. I turn left and start walking toward Bray, away from the busy part of the beach, the part nearest the car parks. *People are so lazy*, I think as I kick some smooth sea-washed pebbles with my toe and make my way toward the water's edge.

I scowl at an old crumbling lump of dog poo and jump over it. Then I push my hands down into the pockets of my jeans and walk faster, the damp, compact sand squeaking a little under my feet.

A black-and-white collie dashes out of the surf in front of me and shakes itself, showering my jeans with salt water. I yelp and step back, but it's too late; I'm soaked.

I look crossly at the boy who's pulling his dog away by the collar.

"Bad dog, Billy," he says. Yikes, it's Seth Stone, from art class. He hasn't recognized me, thank goodness.

But he looks up at me and says, "Sorry." And then, "Amy, hi. How weird."

You're the weirdo, I think, but instead I say, "Hi. Nice dog." *Great, Amy. What an intelligent thing to say.*

"Thanks. This delinquent is Billy." Seth squats down and gives the dog a hug around the neck, leaving a wet patch on his white T-shirt. I try not to stare. He's got a really muscular chest. Who would have thought? He has no time for sports at school: he always ditches PE and hides behind the art studio, listening to his iPod. Everyone knows he's there, even the teachers. I was sent to get him once, but they've pretty much given up on him at this stage.

"I've never seen you down here before," he says, standing up.

I shrug. "My gramps — sorry, grampa — lives up the road. I come here the odd time. When I want to get away from things, clear my head."

Seth nods. "Yeah, I know what you mean." He lets go of Billy's collar, and the dog powers off down the beach toward Dalkey. "Which way are you going?" Seth asks.

I point toward Bray.

"Can we tag along?"

I can hardly say no. "Sure."

Billy is heading the wrong way, so Seth gives a strong, ear-piercing whistle, making me jump and my eardrums ring. Billy stops mid-gallop and does a high-speed turn, legs splayed out like a cartoon dog. He sprints back toward us.

"Sorry," Seth says. "Should have warned you. Polly says I'll deafen someone one day."

Who's Polly? I wonder. *There's no Polly in school. Maybe he has a girlfriend in another school.* For some reason this interests me, but I'm too shy to ask.

"I'd love to be able to do that," I say. "I can't whistle."

Seth grins at me. "Course you can. Everyone can." Billy runs past us, chasing a seagull into the sea.

"I can't. Look." I purse my lips and blow through them. All that comes out is a thin reedy noise, like wind gusting in though the edge of a window. "See?"

"Are you using your tongue *and* your cheeks?" Seth asks.

"I don't know." I purse my lips again and concentrate on what I'm doing.

"You have to use your cheeks like a muscle. Don't leave them all flabby. Tighten them up."

I give it a go. I must look mental.

"Now get some tongue action going."

I laugh and raise my eyebrows. I can't help it. Tongue action?

He smiles and his face lights up. I don't think I've ever seen him smile, not properly. He always looks so sullen, as if he's in pain. Then he looks at me. And I look at him. And there's something there, something I can't explain. A tiny spark. Electricity. Suddenly I notice things I've never noticed before. The way his hair falls over his sky-blue eyes, the smattering of freckles over his nose, his high, angular cheekbones . . .

Seth interrupts my thoughts. "Amy? Are you all right?"

I'm mortified. How long have I been staring at him?

"Sorry," I say. "I was miles away. Trying to concentrate on the whistling." Thank God for Clover's sunglasses. At least he can't see my eyes properly.

"Ah, right. Try again. Tighten up those cheeks, then roll the air along your tongue and out your lips."

I try it, really concentrating this time. And there it is. A whistle! Tiny and birdlike, but a whistle all the same. I grin, delighted with myself. "Ha! I did it!"

Seth grins at me. "Yep. See, told you. Everyone can whistle." His face lights up again. Like Clover, he has a tiny gap between his two front teeth. It's cute. I drag my eyes away and stare at the sea. I really must stop this. It's only Seth Stone. But when he looks at me, I'm starting to get a deliciously warm feeling in the pit of my stomach.

"Race you to the Martello Tower," he says.

"You're on."

Half an hour later, we're still sitting on the beach in front of the round stone tower. Billy is lolling beside us, snoozing. His fur is matted, and he smells a little.

But he's still adorable. I'm wiggling my toes in the warm sand, and Seth is throwing stones into the sea. He's got an amazing throwing arm.

"You should join the cricket team," I say after a particularly good toss.

"With that pack of losers? No thanks." He puts his arms behind him and lies back on them, his back straight. He looks like a triangle.

"You might enjoy it. You'd be a great bowler."

He says nothing for a moment, staring out to sea. "Actually, I tried out for the team."

"When?"

"Ages ago."

"And?"

He shrugs. "Got picked. Never played a game."

"Why not?"

Something flickers over his face. He sits up and begins to rub Billy's tummy. "Family stuff."

"You can tell me. I won't say anything. I'm not a gossip."

"I know *you're* not . . ." he trails off.

"What are you saying?" I ask, offended. "That my friends are gossips? You mean Sophie and Mills, don't you?"

"Don't get all angsty."

"Hey, you've just insulted my best friends."

He just goes on rubbing Billy, his eyes fixed on the dog's tummy.

"Sophie and Mills are really loyal, you know," I continue. "Mills is, anyway. And they never gossip about things that matter."

Seth snorts. "Things that matter? What, like people's feelings? So it's cool for them to slag off emos, then? That's OK?"

"No! You're twisting my words. I just mean —"

"Tell me exactly what you mean, then. Go on. You think I don't know what you lot say about me behind my back? That I'm a weirdo? That my shirts look like I've slept in them? That I look like a vampire? I'm not deaf, Amy. Things at home have been rough, which is why I'm not exactly a ray of sunshine in school. But you and your buddies don't care about things like that, do you? Because it *doesn't matter*." He uses a girlie, singsong voice to say the last two words, and it really gets to me.

I ball my hands into fists. "How dare you?" I'm so annoyed, I could hit him. "My life's not exactly brilliant, either. My dad's having a baby with his secretary. Who I can't stand. And they got married in secret. My mum's in bits about it."

"But she's not dying." As soon as he says the words, the whole world stops.

"What?" I say in a low voice. "Is your mum dying?"

His eyes are still glued to Billy's stomach. "No. She was sick, but she's fine now. I don't know why I said that."

I twist around so I'm kneeling in the sand, facing him. "Are you sure? Do you want to talk about it?"

He looks out to sea again. His mouth is slightly twisted, and I can tell he's upset. He blinks quickly several times. My heart lurches. He looks so sad; his eyes are all stormy, and I have to admit it's very attractive. The tortured artist. *Get a grip, Amy,* I tell myself.

"No, not really," he says. "She had a really bad virus, but they caught it early. She's going to be fine." He pauses and then says, "Look, it's no big deal. Please don't tell anyone in school."

"Do you really think that little of me?"

He shrugs. "I don't know you, Amy. Not really. I like you in art class. But when you're with Mills and Sophie, you're a different person."

"I've been friends with Mills all my life. She lives three doors down from me. We grew up together."

"And Sophie?"

I sigh. "Mills thinks Sophie's great. So I have to hang out with her."

"No, you don't. You have a choice."

"But I'll lose Mills."

"You think she'd pick Sophie over you?"

I nod.

"Not much of a friend, then, is she?" He rubs Billy's belly and combs his curling fur out with his fingers.

"You don't understand."

"No, you're right. I don't." He pauses, then says, "Better get this guy back. Polly will be wondering where we've gotten to." He stands up and hits the back of his black jeans to get rid of the sand. "She worries a bit."

There it is again: Polly. This time I ask, "Who's Polly?"

"My mum."

I stand up and look at him.

"You call her Polly?"

He shrugs. "Sure, it's her name. There's just the two of us; we're pretty tight."

I want to say something, but I'm lost for words. It's clear he worries about her too.

Billy barks, as if telling us to get a move on. He's halfway to the train station by this stage. We start walking toward him.

"Listen, I'm sorry about your family stuff," he says. "It sounds messy."

I smile at him. "I'll live." Then I realize what I've just said. "I'm sorry, I didn't mean . . . Your mum and everything . . . I wasn't thinking. . . ." My words are getting all tangled, like a broken piece of fishing net washed up on the shore.

He gives me a gentle smile. "Hey, it's fine. You're right — you'll live."

I bend down, pick up a smooth, flat shell, and turn it over in my hands. "Clover says once the baby's here, things will settle down. She's my aunt. I just hate it when my parents yell at each other, you know?"

"They yell in front of you?"

"Sometimes. They used to do it all the time, but they don't live together anymore. Mum lives with Dave now. And Dad lives with his secretary. She's much younger than Mum, and it's kinda gross. Mum calls her Little Miss Perky."

Seth smiles. "How old is she?"

"Twenty-nine. Dad's forty-three."

Seth whistles. "Parents are strange, all right." He crosses his eyes, and I laugh.

Just as we reach the bridge, Seth says, "Hey, forgot to say, I like your Bebo site. Cool skin."

"You've seen it?"

He looks away. The tips of his ears have gone crimson.

"Sure," he says. "I'll leave you a message. Hey, you can put me in your top sixteen."

Sophie and Mills will have a fit if I list him as one of my top sixteen friends, but they can just deal with it. Seth's cool. And he likes my site. I start to feel slightly floaty, and I can't stop smiling.

"OK, I will," I say through my smile.

As I walk back toward Gramps's house, I think about Seth and wonder what he really thinks of me. My phone beeps. It's Mills. WHAT'S UP? IN DUNDRUM WITH SOPH AND THE GIRLS. GOT COOL WEDGES IN PENNEYS. SEE YOU IN SCHOOL. XXX

My face drops and I'm glad Seth isn't with me. Mills went to Dundrum with Sophie and the D4s without telling me, let alone asking me. Did Mills text me just to rub it in? Maybe Seth's right. Some friend! But am I strong enough to do anything about it? If I do make her choose between me and Sophie, and she picks Sophie, where does that leave me? Alone. At least this way I have a friend.

♥ Chapter 14

When I get home that night, I expect to find Mum weeping on Dave's shoulder or sitting at the kitchen table shoveling Ben & Jerry's chocolate ice cream into her mouth with a wooden spoon. But instead she's in the sitting room watching *What Not to Wear* with a notebook on her knees.

"Hi, Amy." She looks up as I walk into the room. "How was your day? Sorry about earlier."

"That's OK." I sit down on the arm of the sofa, willing her not to go on and on about the shouting and everything.

"What are you doing?" I ask her as she scribbles *V-neck tops, not round neck* in her notebook.

"I've decided to change my image," she says. "A total makeover. I'm doing my research."

I watch the large lady on the television screen. She's wearing saggy black tracksuit bottoms and a dark purple tank top that is stretched over her huge droopy boobs. The outfit does her no favors. The presenters have their work cut out for them.

"You're much better looking than she is," I say.

"I should hope so. She's a lunch lady in her fifties. I'm not that old." Mum runs her fingers through her long dark-blond hair. It reminds me of Seth combing out Billy's fur.

"Mum, can you die from a virus?"

"A virus? Only if it's a really bad one. You should ask Dave about it; he'd know. Why do you ask?"

"Something I saw on the telly."

"Oh, right." She puts down her pen and pulls her hair back off her head into a loose ponytail with her hands. "Do you think I should get my hair cut short? Would it make me look younger? More trendy?" She lets a few wispy bits hang down. "Should I get layers? Or go super-blond like Clover? What do you think?"

I look at her. I don't want to offend her, but is she delusional? White blond, at her age? She's hardly Madonna. "Maybe a few highlights. I wouldn't do anything drastic. Bleached hair can be very draining."

"Clover gets away with it." She twists the ponytail

and then piles all the hair on top of her head. "Do I look more sophisticated with my hair up?"

I remember Dave telling Dad that she's fragile at the moment, so I don't tell her: one, Clover is a lot younger than she is, and, two, with her hair like that, she's a dead ringer for Bellatrix Lestrange from *Harry Potter.* "Why don't you just get a trim and some highlights?" I say instead. "Like normal."

She blows the air out of her mouth and slumps down on the sofa. "That's just it — I don't want normal. I want something different. Something dramatic. You know, I think I'll go to the hairdresser's tomorrow."

"Don't get anything mental, Mum, like pink hair. It'd be so embarrassing."

"They're professionals, Amy. They're not going to give me pink hair. I'll leave it in their capable hands."

"OK," I say a little doubtfully. "But why don't you ask Clover to go with you?"

"Clover?" Mum sniffs. "I'm sure she's far too busy with her magazine work. Dave's not working till seven tomorrow, so I'll go shopping and get my hair done. Some *me* time." Her eyes glisten with longing. "I can hardly wait."

"Where is she?" Clover asks the following evening. I begged her to come over. Dave's gone out to work, and I don't know what to do. Luckily I've managed to get Evie to sleep, but Alex won't go to bed and is still crawling around the living room in his Thomas the Tank Engine pajamas. Mum's shut herself in her bedroom and won't come out. She was wearing one of Dave's old baseball hats when she came into the house, and I could tell she'd been crying, because her mascara had spidered down her cheeks in black wavy lines.

"In her room," I say.

"I'm going up, Beanie. Probably best if you stay down here." Clover walks up the stairs in her bare feet, wearing a neat yellow hoodie and a tiny pair of white shorts. I wonder absently where she's left her flip-flops. After she's gone into Mum's room, I creep up the stairs and stand with my back against the wall, ready to leap into my own room if I'm caught. I've popped Alex into his playpen with a biscuit in each hand, so hopefully he'll stay quiet for a few minutes.

Mum's door is ajar, and when I peer in, I can see her slumped over the side of the bed, her face in her hands. At least I think it's Mum. Her head is covered in maroon-colored hedgehog spikes. The tips are picked out in lurid purple. If Sharon Osbourne stuck her finger in a plug socket, she'd look like Mum.

"*Siúcra diúcra!*" Clover's hands jump to her mouth. "What have they done to you, Sylvie?" She sits down on the bed beside Mum and puts her arms around her. "Why didn't you tell them to stop?"

"I was reading *25 Beautiful Homes*," Mum says, tears flooding her eyes and rolling down her cheeks. "I never get to read magazines these days, and it was such a treat. When I looked up, she'd already done half my head, so I thought it was better to keep my mouth shut."

Clover picks up a piece of Mum's hair and studies it carefully. "But what about the color? Did you ask for plum?"

"Nooooo," Mum wails. "She said it would suit me."

"Sylvie," Clover says, getting all serious. "What exactly did you tell the hairdresser?"

"I told her I wanted something different, something trendy."

Clover gasps. "You never say 'different' to a hairdresser, Sylvie. It's like a red flag to a bull. They go all *loop-da-loop* if you say 'different.' Remember the time I came home with electric-blue hair? That's what happens if you say 'different' to a hairdresser."

"But you liked your blue hair," Mum says through her tears.

"I know, but that's not the point." Clover takes one of Mum's hands and strokes it, the way you'd stroke a child's hand or a pet rabbit. "You should have asked me to come with you. You know what you're like with hairdressers. I have the same problem with the dentist. I'm terrified of her, especially when she starts pulling at my gums. We're both scared of women in authority; that's our problem."

Mum laughs, and snot comes out her nose. She dabs at it with a crumpled and wet-looking tissue. "You're not scared of anyone, Clover. Even the dentist."

Clover grins at her. "I'm just trying to make you feel better." She looks at the floor, which is littered with shopping bags. "Hey, looks like you've been doing some serious credit-card damage. Can I see?" She picks up a bag and pulls out a gold-sequined dress. It sparkles in the light.

"Cool dress," Clover says, holding it up against her chest.

"Dress?" Mum wrinkles her nose. "I thought it was a top. It's a bit short for a dress."

Clover laughs. "You could wear it over skinny jeans or tight black trousers. Do you have skinny jeans?"

Mum frowns and shakes her head. "You'd better

have it. I won't wear it. I don't know what I was thinking."

Clover pulls out two cardigans from a Topshop bag, one grass green, the other peacock blue. They have lots of pearl buttons the size of golf balls down the front. "Are these both the same?"

"Yes, but in different colors."

"They're not bad, but the buttons are a bit Bobo the Clown."

Mum's shoulders slump. "I thought everything in Topshop was cool and trendy."

Clover says, "I think we need to return some of this, Sylvie. Listen, Beanie and I will go shopping with you. How about Thursday evening in Dundrum? I'm sure we'll find something there."

"Dave's working," Mum says glumly. "And I don't know if I'd have the energy. I'm exhausted after six. I just want my bed."

"Don't be such a party pooper. I'll ask Gramps to babysit, tell him it's an emergency. And tomorrow morning we're going straight back to the hairdresser's. I'm going to give that girl a piece of my mind."

Mum cringes. "Do we have to?"

Clover nods firmly. "Sylvie, you look crazy. Even Meg from the White Stripes wouldn't get away with that hair."

"Who?" Mum isn't all that up on bands. She only discovered the Script last week, after hearing them on the radio. When it comes to music, she's stuck in the eighties.

Clover smiles. "Madonna, OK? Even Madonna wouldn't get away with that hair."

Mum starts to cry again. "I feel like such an idiot."

"It happens to everyone. I'll tell her exactly what to do, and I'll stay and watch so she doesn't go getting any ideas."

Clover is as good as her word. When I get home from school on Tuesday, Mum looks very, very different. But in a good way this time. Her hair is now a delicious honey color, and it's layered around her face, with a wispy fringe. Very sophisticated. It looks a bit funny with her navy T-shirt with baby puke on the shoulder, jeans, and flip-flops.

"Hey, I like the new hair." I throw my bag on the floor beside the kitchen table. "I'm starving. Anything to eat?"

Mum tucks some stray bits of hair behind her ears. "You don't think it's a bit short?"

"No, it's cool. Must have cost you."

"Not a penny. Clover sorted all that out. She gave

the manager a right earful, said she was in half a mind to write about it in her magazine, so they did it for free. She's completely shameless. Luckily the original girl was off, and I had someone different, a man called Freddie. At least I think it was a man. He was wearing makeup, so it was hard to tell. Clover said he looked like the singer from the Scissor Sisters. Are they like Girls Aloud?"

"Kind of." I smile at her. "I wouldn't complain. It obviously worked."

Mum nods. "Now all I need is my new cool and trendy wardrobe. And can you show me how to use the Internet again? I was thinking of buying a Bebo page. Making some new friends."

I give a laugh. "You don't buy them, Mum. It's free."

Her eyes light up. "Really? Even better."

"Why do you want a Bebo page? It's not really for olds."

"Clover has one."

"Mum, she's seventeen. You're nearly forty."

"I'm thirty-seven, thank you very much." Her fingers flutter up to the edges of her eyes. She reaches in her pocket and squeezes a little clear-colored gel onto her fingertips and begins to massage it into her crow's-feet. I read the yellow tube. PREPARATION H.

"What's that?" I ask. It has a very pungent smell. Like cough medicine mixed with Pine-Sol.

"Hemorrhoid cream. It's supposed to be great for wrinkles."

I happen to know that hemorrhoids are things old people get on their bums. It was on *Scrubs* once. "Yuck, gross. Put it away, Mum." She's seriously losing it.

On Wednesday, Mills comes over after school. Sophie is at the orthodontist's, so I think she's at a bit of a loose end.

"I saw you talking to Seth Stone today," Mills says as I click on the computer. Mum is out walking Evie, and Alex is playing with his wooden train set at our feet. I said I'd keep an eye on him. I'm being extra nice to Mum in the hope that she'll buy me some new gear at Dundrum tomorrow.

"Really?" I say. "It was probably something about art homework."

"You looked pretty pally to me." Her eyes narrow. "Is there something you're not telling me?"

I ignore her, log on to my Bebo page, and hope I'm not blushing.

Mills is watching me closely. "Amy! You don't fancy him, do you? He's such a freak."

I spin around. "He's not a freak. If you actually bothered to talk to him, you'd find out he's really nice."

Mills stares at me. "Talk to him? Are you mad? Why would I want to do that? He's an emo, Amy, although he is quite cute, I suppose."

"He's not an emo. He's just himself. People don't have to *be* anything, Mills."

Her eyes widen. "But if you're not in with a crowd, who do you hang out with at lunch and after school?"

She's such an innocent sometimes. And from the sound of things, Sophie has her practically brainwashed.

"Ah, Mills, I'm sick of all this tribal stuff. Crombies, emos, D4s. Why can't we just talk to everyone? You know, you weren't like this before you met Sophie."

"I see." She gives me a smug smile.

"What?"

"You're jealous of Sophie."

"I'm not jealous of Sophie. As if. Don't be daft."

Mills stares at my Bebo page. "What's with the new skin? It's a bit gloomy."

I've used a red-and-black Rothko painting as my new skin. I suppose it is a bit dark, but I like it.

127 ♥

Alex starts to call. "Da, da, da, da." He sticks out his little arms and looks up at me hopefully.

"What does he want?" Mills asks.

"To be picked up. Would you mind? He might need to be changed."

Mills picks him up reluctantly. I stick my nose in his bottom and sniff.

"Gross!" Mills says. "What are you doing?"

"Seeing if his nappy's full."

"If it is, you're on your own."

"Don't be such a wuss. Anyway, you're in luck. No poop."

Alex is wriggling around in Mills's arms.

"What do I do with him?" she asks.

I sigh, standing up. "Here, I'll take him." He clings to me like a bush baby.

Mills hops onto my chair and starts to read my Bebo site.

"Why is Seth one of your friends?"

I shrug. "He asked me."

"And what's this? 'I hate D4s who hang out in herds in Dundrum and say "Oh, my God" all the time. I call them "Oh, My Goddesses. All surface and no substance." What does that mean? 'All surface and no substance'?"

"Exactly what it says. That they're self-obsessed and shallow."

She scowls at me. "Do you think I'm shallow?"

Before I have a chance to say no, she jumps up.

"I thought we were friends, Amy. You know, I spend most of my time defending you to the girls. Saying what fun you are, how they should give you a chance. But all the time you've been mouthing off about me behind my back. Well, thanks a lot, Amy. Thanks for nothing." She runs out of the room, and the next thing I hear is the front door bang. I'd go after her, but Alex is still on my hip.

I feel like crying. Great, now I've lost my best friend. And it's all my own stupid fault. I was trying to be clever, and, if I'm honest, I was trying to impress Seth. I should have kept my mouth and my Bebo site firmly shut.

I get Alex a teething biscuit and a sippy cup of juice and then I settle down to IM Seth. At least he's still talking to me.

I've just had a huge fight with Mills, I type. *Bummer.*

Want some company? he writes back immediately.

I think about it for a second. *Do you like babies? Love them. Especially with ketchup.*

♥ Chapter 15

When the doorbell rings half an hour later, I'm in the middle of changing Alex's nappy. I give his bum cheeks one last swipe and throw the yucky baby wipe into a plastic bag.

"Stay put, buster," I tell him. I grab another wipe, clean my hands, and run into the hall.

"Sorry, Seth," I say, opening the door, a smile plastered on my face. Even the thought of Seth makes me feel better. "I'm just changing—" I stop suddenly. It's not Seth on the doorstep; it's Mills.

I stand there for a few seconds, not knowing what to say. Eventually I manage, "Oh, hi."

"Hi," she says back. She's holding her hands in front of her and twisting them around, the way she always does when she's nervous. "I just wanted to—"

Just then Seth cycles up the path on a black mountain bike. The back tire is a bit flat. His cheeks are flushed, and his hair is windswept. I can't help but grin. He looks so cute.

Mills turns, looks at him and then back at me. She's not smiling. She raises her eyebrows. "I can see you're busy." She must think I was lying to her about Seth all along, which I was, I suppose.

I say, "Mills, wait," but then Alex comes waddling out of the living room, his bum naked to the world.

"Da, da, da," he says, clearly delighted with himself. He's got the dirty nappy in one hand and is trailing it behind him by one of its sticky tabs like a dog on a leash. Luckily I'd folded it into a parcel, so nothing evil is escaping. But the musky, sweet stench of baby poo fills the hall.

"Alex!" I yell, pulling the nappy out of his hand. "Gross."

I turn around to talk to Mills, but she's halfway down the path. Seth says, "Hiya, Mills," to her, and she gives him a rather curt "Hi" back.

"Mills!" I shout after her. "I'll come over later, OK? When Mum's back."

"Don't bother," she says without turning around. "I'm going out with Sophie and the girls."

"What was all that about?" Seth asks. He gets

off his bike and props it against the wall under the living-room window.

"Do you have a lock?" I ask, putting the nappy in the wheelie bin. I don't want to talk to Seth with a steaming nappy in my hand. He might think the yang is me.

"No," he says.

"Better put it around the back, then. The side gate's open." I point to the right of the house.

"Amy, is the baby allowed out there?" Seth asks. I follow his gaze.

Alex is sitting on the patch of rough grass on the pavement at the side of the road. He's picking daisies and eating them. I shriek, then run out and scoop him up in my arms. "Bad baby." I put my little finger into his mouth and hook out half a daisy head. I hope they're not poisonous. He gives me a nip with his new front teeth for my trouble. "Ow! Alex!"

Seth is watching me, laughing.

Then I feel a warm sensation down the front of my jeans. Alex has only gone and peed all over me. That's all I need. I walk back into the house, holding him out in front of me, his legs waggling around like a rag doll's.

"I'll have to change," I tell Seth. "Sorry."

He shrugs. "No problem. Give him to me, and I'll put a nappy on his butt. Where are they?"

"Are you sure?" I stare at him.

"Sure. I have loads of nieces and nephews that age. I'm always helping out. What is he, one?"

"One and a half." I blow a raspberry on Alex's neck. He loves it. Right on cue, he gives a hiccupy giggle. "This is Alex. Alex, meet Seth."

"Hi, Alex." Seth takes one of Alex's little hands and shakes it.

So cute. I beam at Seth. In fact, I'm having a hard time not smiling like a circus clown. It's so lovely to see him. He wasn't in school on Tuesday afternoon for some reason, so he missed art class. And I missed him. I haven't been talking to him at break. I usually eat lunch sitting on the steps by the science labs with Sophie and Mills. To be honest, I have no idea where Seth has lunch. I've never really thought about it.

When I come back downstairs, Seth and Alex have disappeared. For a split second, I panic. Maybe Seth's run off with the baby. You hear about things like that on the news. Maybe his mum can't have any more children and . . .

Then I hear Alex screaming. It's coming from the

garden. I watch from the kitchen window as Seth speeds around the grass with Alex in his arms. Alex is grinning and giggling. He's flapping his chubby arms up and down like a baby bird learning to fly. He looks so content. I feel a lurch of happiness in the pit of my stomach, and I stand, spying on them, until I'm spotted.

"Hey, Amy!" Seth shouts. "We're being a shark. Come on in; the water's lovely."

When Mum comes home, we're in the living room messing with my Bebo site. Seth's showing me some really cool YouTube clips, and we've already added one to my flash box: this wild animal fight at a water hole in Africa called "Battle at Kruger." A baby buffalo is grabbed by lions and crocodiles and then gets saved by his herd.

"Hi," Mum says, looking at Seth curiously and then back at me.

"This is Seth," I tell her. "A friend from school."

"Hello, Mrs. Green," he says, jumping to his feet ultra-politely. He looks like he's about to stick out his hand to shake hers.

Mum smiles at him in a friendly sort of way. "I'm not actually Mrs. Green anymore."

Seth's face falls. "Oh, sorry."

"Not a problem. Just call me Sylvie. And it's nice to meet you, Seth." Mum bends down and picks up Alex, who is playing with his Fisher-Price garage, which really means rolling all the cars under the sofa and trying to crawl under to fetch them. He always gets stuck because his nappy gives him a huge sumo wrestler's bum. "Thanks for keeping an eye on this little monster. Was he good?"

"He was fine," I say. "Apart from weeing all over my jeans."

She laughs. "Anyway, you're off the hook now. Evie's asleep in her pram. Try not to wake her up."

"OK. Mum, can I take the laptop upstairs?"

"Of course. But keep the door open." She grins. "I know all about you teenagers and your hopping hormones. I watch *The OC*."

"Mum!" I say, mortified. "*The OC* finished years ago."

"Oh, I must be watching repeats. They show it on one of the satellite channels at six in the morning when I'm up with Evie. Hey, there's a Seth in that too, isn't there? Any relation?"

I groan. "Mum. That's feeble." *Please be quiet and stop embarrassing me*, I plead telepathically.

"I'm only kidding," she says. She's in a very good mood for some reason, which is great. I hope it lasts until tomorrow: shopping-with-Clover day. If she stays so cheery, I might just get new boots *and* new jeans.

Actually, she could have been even more uncool; I've never had a boy in my bedroom before. A proper boy, I mean, not one of my cousins or Dave or my dad. But I know if we stay downstairs, we'll end up looking after Alex again.

Seth walks into my bedroom and looks around, taking in my Jackson Pollock splatter print, *Alchemy*, 1947. Dad got it for me at the Guggenheim Museum in New York. He went with Shelly. The whole trip was wasted on her, of course; all she wanted to do was shop. He says he'll take me there someday, but I'm not holding my breath.

"Hey," Seth says. "The walls aren't pink."

"What were you expecting? Barbie's Magical Kingdom?"

He smiles and then stares at my Georgia O'Keeffe print of a bright red poppy. "But that is a bit girlie. Polly would like it."

"Hey, just because I don't have Munch's *The Scream* on my walls." I run my finger over the poppy's lush black center. "Actually, I used to, but it gave me nightmares."

He laughs. "I know what you mean." He puts his

hands on either side of his head, makes his mouth into a long *O*, and twists his body, giving a very good impression of the painting. "Turn off that Britney Spears music, or my head's going to fall off," he says in this crazy, ghoulish voice.

I start laughing, and within seconds I can't stop. I get these terrible giggling fits sometimes, often when I'm nervous. Tears are streaming down my face, and I'm finding it hard to breathe properly. It's so embarrassing. I'm laughing so much my stomach muscles are starting to cramp.

"It wasn't that funny," Seth says. "Wait till you see me do Picasso's *Guernica*."

I sit down on the bed, gulping for air like a guppy fish and holding my aching stomach.

"Sorry, sorry," he says. "Try thinking of something sad."

I take another raggedy breath, and Shelly's face floats in front of my eyes. I had a laughing fit the first time I met her. It was awful. We were in an Italian restaurant in Dalkey, the kind with checked tablecloths and real Italian waiters in very tight black trousers. Shelly kept giggling and flirting with one of them, a curly-haired man in his twenties with a gold Saint Christopher medallion nestling in his black chest hairs.

I remember thinking it was a bit off. Wasn't she supposed to be in *luurve* with my dad? She'd split Mum and Dad up, so it had better have been for a good reason. I looked at Shelly, really looked at her. I suppose I could see the attraction if you liked that kind of thing—obvious—blond flicky hair, skinny white jeans, and dazzling teeth the size of piano keys. She was also a lot younger than Mum and a lot more glam.

I was really nervous, and then Dad made this lame waiter joke.

"A guy goes into a restaurant, looks at the menu, and asks the waiter, 'How do you prepare your chickens?' And the waiter says, 'We just tell them straight out that they're going to die.'"

See, told you it was lame. It was so lame, I started laughing and I just couldn't stop. Shelly pushed my glass of Coke toward me and said, "Try taking a sip." So I did, but the bubbles went the wrong way, and I ended up snorting it all over the tablecloth and all over Shelly. I was mortified. Shelly had to excuse herself to wipe snorted Coke off her bare arm.

Dad gave me a quick smile and said, "Don't worry; it could happen to anyone," but from the way he was dabbing at the table with paper napkins, sighing, and making a funny clicking noise with his tongue, like a tap dripping, I could tell he was annoyed with me. When Shelly came back, Dad told me they were moving in together. Mum and Dad had only been separated for two months. Two months! Officially, that is. I'd heard Mum talking to a friend on the phone and saying she figured they'd been at it for a lot longer. Something to do with Dad joining the gym and buying new boxer shorts and aftershave.

I just stared at Dad. Luckily my pizza arrived, so I didn't have to say anything. It was a very quick meal.

Thinking of that day, the bubble bursts and I stop laughing. Seth must think I'm such a sap.

"I'm so sorry," I say, still a little breathless.

"Hey, don't worry about it. I'm a funny guy."

I smile at him. "You look more like a mushroom to me. Get it, fun-gi?"

Seth groans and rolls his eyes.

I'm dreading seeing Mills in school tomorrow. I tried ringing her after Seth left, but she wasn't answering her mobile, and when I rang her house, her mum, Sue, said she couldn't come to the phone right now.

"Is she still annoyed with me?" I asked. You can ask her things like that. Sue's a bit mumsy, always making flat fairy cakes that you can only get your teeth into when they're hot, but generally she's cool.

"Yes. Give her till tomorrow. I'm sure she'll have calmed down by then."

Calmed down? That didn't sound good.

♥ Chapter 16

Mills and I are in different classes on Thursday mornings, so I don't see her till break. As I walk toward the science lab steps, I spot her sitting with Sophie, their heads bent together, chatting intensely. We always hang out and eat here when it's cold or raining (which, being Ireland, it usually is!). Otherwise we're outside working on our tans, and in Sophie's case, showing off rather a lot of leg. She thinks they're fit, but she's delusional.

The steps are covered with gray carpet tiles to match the gray walls. Being in school is depressing enough: you'd think the designers would have injected some blue or green or red into the equation.

But oh, no, Saint John's is fully mouse-grayed-up from floor to ceiling.

Different groups and years hang out in different areas of the school. Except the emos. I never see them at lunch, which is strange. Maybe they go underground, like moles.

Mills and Sophie both look up and stare at me silently, looking slightly guilty. I get the feeling they were just talking about me.

"Hi, Mills. Hi, Sophie," I say. I'm really nervous, and I can hear my heart pounding in my ears. *Stop it,* I tell myself. *It's only Mills and Sophie.*

Sophie drops her chin and gives me a bemused look. "We thought you'd be in Emo Land," she says. "With your *boyfriend.*" She gives me a twisted smile.

"He's not my boyfriend," I say.

"Ooooh, get her," Sophie says to Mills. "That's what they all say. Is he a good snog? Or is his lipstick a bit sticky?"

I glare at her. "He doesn't wear lipstick. And how should I know? We're just friends."

"Friends?" Mills says. "Like us, Amy?" She seems upset.

"Yeah," Sophie says. "Or are you going to dump him too when someone better comes along? How about Simon Debrett? You'd dump Seth for Si, wouldn't you?"

She starts cackling, like a Disney wicked stepmother.

I stare at Mills. She's not sticking up for me like she usually does. I must have really upset her yesterday. If only Sophie would just disappear so I could talk to her alone. I close my eyes for a second, willing it to happen, but it doesn't.

Instead Sophie grins and says, "Speak of the devil, would you look who it is?" She points down the corridor. Three fifth-year boys are walking toward us.

Oh, no. My stomach does a nervous flip. I look down at the floor and cup my hand around my eyes, willing her to shut up. "Shush, Sophie."

But it's no use; she's on a roll. I have to hide, quick. I jump up and push open the door of the biology lab. Luckily it's unlocked, and I dash inside, closing it behind me. The room smells of formaldehyde — the last class must have been dissecting cow hearts or something. The acrid smell isn't helping my already churning stomach.

I press my ear to the crack between the door and the wall.

"Hi, Si," I hear Sophie say.

"Uh, hi," he says. It's clear he has no idea who Sophie is but doesn't want to be rude. I hear the two boys with him laugh.

"Who's that, dude?" one asks.

"I'm a friend of Amy's," Sophie says. "You know Amy. The girl in first year who fancies you, Si. She's goalie on the Minor A's. In fact, she's hiding in the biology lab."

The boys start to laugh and nudge Simon in the side. "Woo-hoo," they tease. "First-year Crushville. You're the man, Si. Go get her."

I leap back from the door in fright and screw my eyes shut. *Oh, no, please don't . . .* I think I'm going to puke. I put my hands to my burning cheeks in an effort to cool them down.

I hear the door creak, and when I open my eyes, Simon is standing in front of me. I'm so mortified I could cry. But he gives me a gentle smile and mouths "hi" and then walks back out again, closing the door behind him.

"Nice try," he says to Sophie. "I think you're hallucinating; there's no one there. See you around."

Hearing them leave, I open the door a smidge. Simon is walking away quickly, his friends following behind him.

"What was that about, Si?" one asks.

"Just some silly first-year messing," he says. "Pay no attention."

They look at him admiringly. "You're such a ledge."

I'm so relieved. After a few minutes, I go back out and sit on the steps, my heart still pounding. Then I smile to myself. Simon lied to his friends for me. *For me.*

I look up. Sophie is standing in front of me, her hands on her hips. The right-hand side of her skirt is tucked into her knickers at the back, showing off a dimpled white thigh. She must have only fake-tanned the lower half of her legs. I open my mouth to warn her, but before I get a chance, she says, "You think you're so great, don't you? He just felt sorry for you. You heard what he said: you're just a silly first-year."

I stand up and look her in the eye. "He was talking about you, Sophie, not me."

"Yeah, right." Her face is twisted, and I've never seen her look so nasty, even when she's picking on the emo girls. "Look, Amy, I know you and Mills are neighbors, but she doesn't want to hang around with you anymore. Get it? She's sick of you and your moaning." She purses her lips and drops her chin. "Poor liddle me, my mummy can't keep her knickers on, so I have to babysit all the time."

Mills gasps. "Sophie!"

"What?" Sophie demands. "It's true. My mum says normal people don't have sex for at least three months after they've had a baby. She says Amy's mum should have taken precautions; it's dangerous to have two babies so close together."

I've met Sophie's mum a few times, and funnily enough I can imagine her saying just this through her pale wormy lips. She was probably fingering the pearls around her neck at the time. She's always fiddling with her pearls; you'd think they were rosary beads the way she plays with them.

I want to say something, to defend Mum, but I can't. I'm too shocked.

"That's not Amy's fault," Mills says.

"Don't you go sticking up for her." Sophie glares at Mills, and Mills backs off. "She was slagging you off on her Bebo site, remember? Saying you're shallow."

"I wasn't talking about Mills," I say. "You know that, don't you?" I look at Mills. She holds my gaze for a moment and then looks down at the floor. "And would you stop going on about my mum, Sophie? At least she *has* a sex life. At least she's not a withered old bag like your mum."

Sophie's mouth drops open, her braces glittering in the light. Oops, now I've done it. I step backward and stumble into Mr. Olen, my art teacher.

"Is everything all right, girls?" he asks suspiciously, looking from me to Sophie and Mills and then back again.

"Yeah," we all mutter.

The bell rings, but not one of us moves.

"Well, go on," he says with a toss of his head. "Into class. Amy, you're in art with me now, aren't you?"

"Yes, sir."

"*Mark*, Amy, it's Mark. 'Sir' makes me sound so old. You can help me carry down some of the new canvases. They're in a box at the back of the physics lab. We don't have room for them in the studio. Get a move on." He's not budging until I do.

I want to say something to Mills, but I know it's useless. Sophie links her arm. "Have a nice *life*, Amy," she says, and they walk away together.

♥ Chapter 17

That evening I don't feel like doing anything, but Mum pokes her head around my door just after six.

"Ready, Amy?"

She has a big smile on her face and is wearing her good jeans, Sevens that Clover bought her on eBay for her last birthday. Clover said Mum's old Levi 501s were probably as ancient as the original ones worn by the gold prospectors. Did you know American prospectors invented jeans? I certainly didn't. Clover's a mine of useless information like that.

Mum is also wearing green canvas platform sandals, a white V-necked T-shirt, and a denim jacket. Since she spends her life in tracksuits these days, on account of Evie's puking, it's quite a surprise. She actually looks quite nice for an old.

"I think I'll stay here," I say, my eyes a little bleary. I hope she doesn't notice.

I've been lying on my bed, looking up at the stars that Mills gave me for my thirteenth birthday. They used to glow in the dark, but they've faded a bit now. She snuck into my room when I was staying with Dad — Mum let her in and got her the stepladder — and stuck them onto the ceiling. Not in any old way either; she took a book out of the library especially. I now have my own mini-constellation up there: Taurus the Bull. I was really touched. She must have gotten a crick in her neck sticking the stars up in the right order.

"It's your star sign," Mills said as we lay on my bed, side by side, with the curtains closed and the lights off, staring up at them. "To watch over you and keep you safe while you're thirteen."

I'm not really into star signs, but Mills is. If her "horror-scope" tells her to do something, she will. She even faked a sick day on Friday the thirteenth last month. She'd heard an American astrologist on the radio news saying that it was the unluckiest day he'd ever come across in his whole career. Something to do with the stars lining up in a funny way. She stayed in bed all day, worrying. We had double Irish class that day since the English teacher was out sick. Which was very, very bad luck, because Mr. Roley, our pointy-bearded Irish teacher who stinks of BO, is such a bore. So maybe Mills was on to something.

I used to laugh at her superstitions — saluting at single magpies, not walking under ladders, worrying about crossed sticks, jumping over cracks in the pavement — but now I figure, to each their own. If it makes her happy . . .

That's why my eyes are a bit bleary. Mills. I don't know how I'm going to cope in school without her.

"Don't be daft. It's all arranged," Mum says. "Clover will be here in a second." She hesitates. "Are you going in your uniform?"

"'Course not." I sit up too quickly, and my head spins a little. I'll go if it involves getting new gear, I decide. There's an end-of-term party in a few weeks, and I have nothing to wear. My Uggs look a bit sad. I got them last year, and I've worn them to death. I chance my luck. "I really need new boots. The soles have nearly gone on my old ones."

"I can get them re-soled for you," Mum says.

She doesn't get it. I roll my eyes. "Mum!"

She smiles at me. "We'll see, OK?"

The doorbell rings. "That'll be Clover," Mum says. "See you downstairs in a few minutes."

I scramble into my clothes and pull my Uggs over my feet. They're looking saggier by the minute, like a Saint Bernard's face. My boots, that is, not my feet.

As we pull into the brightly lit car park at Dundrum Shopping Centre, Clover asks, "Anything wrong, Beanie? You're very quiet."

"No. I'm just tired. And fed up with studying for exams. We have the day off tomorrow, and I'm going to spend the whole morning in bed."

"Lucky you," she says. "Right, look out for spaces, everyone." Clover's wheels make loud squeaking noises as she takes the car park bends too quickly. The noise makes my teeth feel all funny, like fingernails on a blackboard.

"Clover!" Mum says. "Slow down."

"I see one," Clover says, ignoring Mum and powering toward an empty space. A large black Lexus SUV speeds toward it from the opposite end of the car park. It's farther away than we are, but it's taking no prisoners. It tears into the space so close to Clover's Mini, it nearly clips her front light.

Clover mutters something rude and rests her arm on the horn. *PARP, PARP.* A blond woman with a wrinkly brown neck winds down her window. Oversize designer sunglasses nestle in her perfectly ironed hair, and she's wearing a string of creamy pearls. She oozes money. She bellows, "What's your problem?" Her facial muscles don't even twitch.

"So sorry," Clover says calmly. "I didn't realize you were a senior citizen. Go ahead. Take my space."

The woman's pouty mouth drops, and she gulps a few times, like a pelican swallowing down a fish. Before she has a chance to say anything, Clover drives off, giggling to herself.

"Hope she doesn't come looking for you," Mum says, sounding worried.

Clover just grins. "What can she do? Bash me over the head with her padded Chanel bag? Dig her false nails into me?"

"She could stab you with her Botox syringes," I say. "She probably has a stash of them in her handbag."

Clover laughs. "Good one, Beanie. But she's not going to waste them on me. She's clearly addicted to the stuff. Did you know it comes from a cow's bottom?"

"Really?" I say. "Yuck!"

Mum stares out her passenger window, shaking her head a little. I can tell she's biting the inside of her cheek because her mouth looks all distorted. She reminds me of a disapproving teacher.

"Lighten up, Sylvie," Clover says. "She deserved

it. This place is full of women like that. I think they breed them in the air-conditioning system. You have to stick up for yourself."

"I guess you're right." Mum looks down at her jeans. "I'm glad I dressed up, in that case."

"Dressed up?" Clover laughs. "Sis, we're in Dundrum. Yummy Mummyville. You ain't seen nothing yet."

Mum drags us into the kids' H&M first.

"Sylvie," Clover complains, "we're supposed to be getting clothes for you, not for the babies."

Mum gives a sheepish smile. "I know, I know, but it just called to me as I was walking past." She runs her hands over a tiny pair of jeans. "Look at these. So cute."

"They're a bit small for Alex," I say. "Listen, Mum. Have a quick look around, and then you can come back later, while Clover and I grab a smoothie or something."

But she's in another world, walking through the racks of dinky baby clothes. From the spaced-out look on her face, you'd swear she was having a religious experience.

"Jeepers, Sylvie, you're not preggers again, are you?" Clover says suddenly.

Mum swings around. "What? Pregnant? Of course not. Evie's only three months old. I'm not mad."

Sophie's words ring in my ears. "You were pregnant when Alex was only two months, Mum, weren't you?"

"Yes." Mum puts a pink-and-white cotton shirt back on the rack. "Yes, I was. But that was different."

"Why was it different?" I ask her. She's being a bit cagey, and I really want to know. Was Sophie's mum right? Is Mum irresponsible?

"Do we have to talk about this now, in the middle of H&M?" Mum says.

"Yes!" I say.

She grabs my arm and pulls me toward the back of the shop, where it's quieter. Clover follows closely behind us. I can tell she's as curious as I am.

Mum says, "I suppose I should have told you this before now. But I wasn't sure if you'd understand. Before Alex, I'd wanted a baby for ages, but nothing was happening. So I took some medicine to help things along."

"Clomid?" Clover says.

"Yes," says Mum, surprised.

Clover knows *everything*. We're both staring at her.

She shrugs. "What? I read about it in *Grazia*. One of the stars was talking about it."

Mum continues, "Even then it took ages to get pregnant. So afterward we presumed, you know . . ." A pink blush spreads over Mum's cheeks.

"You didn't think you'd be able to get knocked up again," Clover says helpfully. "But, hey, presto, along came Evie to prove you wrong."

Mum smiles gratefully. "Something like that. It was amazing, like a miracle. We were in complete shock." She rubs her lips together, making a little snapping noise. "So there you have it. Two babies in a year."

"Irish twins," Clover says with a laugh.

I'm lost for words. Hearing about my mum's sex life is a bit embarrassing, to be honest, but I'm glad she's told me. It makes sense now. And Sophie's mum is wrong — Mum's not irresponsible; it was an accident. Like she said, a miracle. You know, I'm glad I asked.

"Anyway," Mum says, "none of this is anything to worry about. We won't be having any more babies, Amy. I promise."

That's a relief. I might get my life back in, say, twelve years. "Can we talk about something else now?" I ask. "Please?"

"Of course." Mum steers me toward the entrance, a hand on my shoulder. "Now, where can we buy those boots you're after?"

She's obviously feeling a bit guilty for making me cringe back there. But if it gets me new Ugglies, then hey, it's so worth it.

♥ Chapter 18

"Do you know those girls?" Clover asks as we're sitting in Fitzpatrick's shoe shop, waiting for a shop
assistant. Mum's looking at some glittery gold sandals beside us, holding them up to the light and
watching them gleam, like Dorothy in *The Wizard of
Oz* with her ruby slippers. She really should get out
more often.

There's a skulk of girls standing at the far end of
the shop, heads together, giggling and staring over at
me. It's Sophie's D4 gang, but she's not with them,
thank goodness.

"Kind of," I say. "They're in my year."

Clover glares at one of them: Nina Pickering.
Nina's wearing a denim mini and a white midriff,

with acres of jangling gold chains around her waist, like a belly dancer; her hip bones stick out of her skin, like a look-at-how-little-I-eat badge of honor. Nina gasps at Clover's audacity and then nudges Annabelle Hamilton, or "Hammy," as Seth calls her because her cheeks are a bit chubby, like a hamster's. Nina whispers something in her ear.

"Oh, *that's* Amy." Annabelle has a plummy voice that carries. "Sophie was right. What a loser: shopping with her mum. And what *is* she wearing?"

I cringe inwardly and stare down at the floor.

"Right," Clover says under her breath. I look up, and she's already in front of Annabelle.

"Clover!" I hiss, but it's too late. Luckily Mum's busy studying the soles of a pair of tall chestnut Uggs.

"Hi, *gurls*," Clover says in a brilliant American drawl, sticking out her hand and curling her lips into a pout. "I'm Roxie Baxter, Star Casting Agency, Noo Yawk. And Amy's second cousin once removed. I'm in Dublin casting a teen movie and catching up with my Irish relatives."

Annabelle's so shocked, she shakes Clover's hand and gives her a huge look-at-my-teeth smile. Annabelle has the best teeth in our year, in the whole school, in fact; I'd like to say they are fake porcelain veneers, but unfortunately they're real. "Annabelle H-H-H-amilton," she stammers. "I take drama classes."

Clover clasps her other hand around Annabelle's, squeezes, and then lets go. "Is that right?" she says. "Well, honey, I'm looking for actors with a bit of character, know what I'm saying? Actors who aren't afraid to show their emotions, who can bark like a dog, squeal like a pig. . . . It's a new teen comedy series set in the Alaskan wilderness, lots of huskies and heaps of snow."

Annabelle's eyes light up. "I can bark like a dog," she says eagerly. Then she starts to bark, *"YAP, YAP, YAPPETY, YAP."* It's actually quite impressive.

"That's a bit too Lassie," Clover says. "I'm looking for something wilder; give me husky, Annabelle, not Labradoodle." I can tell Clover's trying to keep a straight face.

"RRRAAWW, RRRAAAW," Annabelle says.

The whole shop is staring at her, including Mum. Annabelle seems oblivious, her sights set on the Hollywood Hills.

"Now pretend you're tearing into a piece of reindeer meat," Clover says. "I want emotion, Annabelle. Untamed, wild, free."

GNASH, GNASH. Annabelle twists her head from side to side, bearing her perfect molars.

"Good. Now down on all fours," Clover says. She presses her lips together firmly and digs her nails into her hand to stop herself laughing.

And like a good little doggy, Annabelle drops onto her hands and knees and starts crawling around on the floor, barking and tossing her head.

Her friends stare at her in amazement.

Clover takes out her mobile phone and begins to record Annabelle's canine antics. "Awesome, Annabelle. Show me those teeth. Now you're chasing a rabbit; run, Annabelle, run." Clover picks up an Ugg boot from the display and throws it on the wooden floor. "Now, fetch."

Annabelle races up and down the shop on her hands and feet, with an Ugg boot in her mouth.

"Hey," a spotty male shop assistant says, "there'd better not be teeth marks on that boot, or you're paying for it."

"Now, sit," Clover says, ignoring him. "And paw." She holds out her hand. Annabelle is kneeling in front of Clover, her tongue lolling around in her mouth, her "paw" in Clover's hand. I hate to admit it, but she makes a pretty good dog.

Clover drops Annabelle's "paw" and gives her a knowing smile. She flicks her mobile shut and tucks it into her bra cup.

"Allow me to introduce myself," she says in her normal voice. "I'm not Roxie Baxter at all. I'm Clover Wildgust, a friend of Amy's. And if you ever, ever pick on Amy or any of her friends again, I'll put this doggy clip on Bebo. And I'll print a picture of you being Fido in my magazine. Do you understand?"

"Y-y-y-ou're not a casting agent?" Annabelle stammers.

"Not yet," Clover says. "It's on my list. At the moment I'm a journalist on the *Goss*."

Several of the girls gasp.

"I love the *Goss*," Nina simpers. She gazes at Clover in admiration.

"Do you understand me?" Clover asks Annabelle in a clipped voice.

"Yes," Annabelle says. She catches my eye and glares at me.

Clover pats her hidden mobile and raises her eyebrows. "Hello? You're forgetting something, doggy girl. Apologize to Amy."

"Sorry, Amy." Annabelle gives me a fake smile that doesn't reach her eyes.

"That's better," Clover says. "Nice doing business with you."

Annabelle flounces off, followed by her pack, all tittering behind her back. She rounds on them with an iceberg look, but I know it's going to be all over the school by Monday. Nina has a notoriously big mouth.

"Tell me if you have any more trouble with Annabelle or any of her mini hags, OK, Beanie?" Clover says.

"What was that all about?" Mum says.

Clover shrugs. "Just something for the magazine. On your favorite animal."

"Gosh," Mum says staring at Annabelle's disappearing back, "that girl took it very seriously, didn't she?"

Clover says, "Yep. Now which Uggly boots are you after, Beanie?"

"The chestnut ones." I point at a pair of tall Uggs.

"Good choice." She nods in agreement. "They don't get as grubby as the sand ones."

"Amy, they're so expensive," Mum says. "Can't you get a pair in Penneys or something?"

"No, Mum, they're not the same. The cheap ones go funny at the back, like an elephant's knees. Uggs last for ages. I've had these ones for nearly a year, remember? And I wear them all the time."

"I suppose." She isn't convinced.

"I'll go halves with you, Sylvie," Clover says, taking out her wallet and looking in it. "Oops, make that a quarter."

"Please? I've been helping with the babies a lot," I say hopefully. "And I'll put some of my birthday money toward it. I still have thirty euros left."

Mum smiles. "Oh, go on, then. But they'd better last you."

"Thanks, Mum," I say. "You're the best."

Clover gives a little cough. "Ahem."

I grin. "You too, Clover."

Dave nearly collapses when he sees the multicolored fan of shopping bags in each of our hands.

"How much did you spend?" he asks Mum.

Mum waves her hand in front of her face and giggles. Her cheeks are flushed. She dumps her shopping bags at the bottom of the stairs, almost falling over one in the process.

"Have you been drinking?" Dave stares at her. "Sylvie, you're breastfeeding! What about Evie?"

After shopping, Mum treated us all to pizza in Milano's, and as she wasn't driving for a change, she had two glasses of wine. Clover practically forced them on her.

"Go on, Sylvie, live a little," Clover had said.

But Mum's not used to drinking, and I think it's gone to her head.

Clover looks a little guilty. "I have to run. Thanks for the pizza, Sylvie. Talk to you tomorrow." She skips out the door.

"Look at my new underwear," Mum says, and lifts up her top to show Dave her lacy pink bra. She liked it so much, she changed into it in the pizza place and insisted on wearing it home. "Isn't it sexy?"

"Mum!" I say, horrified. "Pull your T-shirt down."

Dave is just staring at Mum as she shimmies and trips around the hall. At first he looks a bit shocked, but then his mouth twitches into a smile and his eyes start to shine. *Eeeuw!* Get me out of here.

"'Night," I say. "I'm off to bed." But they completely ignore me. They're staring at each other as if they've just met. I live in a madhouse.

♥ Chapter 19

We have no school on Friday since there's a teachers' meeting in the morning and an important soccer
match against Monkstown College in the afternoon.
I was looking forward to hanging out with Mills,
but the way things are, that's not going to happen.
She's probably off to jiggle around on the sidelines
in her hitched-up field hockey skirt with the other
D4s to "support" the boys and to distract the opposi-
tion — it's an old Saint John's tactic. It only works on
the teams from all-boys' schools.

I rack my brains. Who can I hang out with? Who
has less than no interest in soccer? Then it comes to
me. Seth! But then I remember. I was pretty shabby
to him yesterday in art class. I was upset about Mills

and Sophie and took it out on him. Stupid, stupid, stupid. Now I have zero friends. Unless . . .

This can't be the place. There's graffiti everywhere, and rubbish lies in layers against the concrete wall surrounding the low-rise flats, like a crisp-packet snowdrift. A beer bottle rolls gently in the wind at the bottom of the steps to the ground-floor flats, making a hollow ringing noise.

I read Seth's text again. NUMBER 3, EDEN HEIGHTS, BALLYVALE. This is Eden Heights, all right. I scan the row of doors on the ground floor, and then I find it, number 3 — glossy red, you can't miss it. It's the only door that isn't faded and cracked. The only door that actually has a number on it.

I ring the bell. I hear muffled voices, and then the door swings open. Seth is standing there, his face expressionless, his hand still on the latch.

"This had better be good," he says. Then he turns away from me. "Polly, I'm going out," he calls, and goes to shut the door behind him. But she's too quick.

"Bring your friend in, Seth," she says. "I'd like to meet him."

"Him?" I whisper.

Seth rolls his eyes. "Pay no attention — my mum's a bit loco."

"Listen," I say before I chicken out. "I'm so sorry about yesterday. About art class. Mills and Sophie were horrible to me at break, and I took it out on you." I hand him the sea-green shopping bag from the bookshop. "I got this for you. Peace offering."

He takes the bag from me, pulls out the large paperback, and strokes the cover with his hand. *Rothko at the Guggenheim*. This must have cost a fortune. Thanks, Amy." He can't help but smile.

I'm so glad he likes it. I had to borrow the money off Dave — Mum never has any money in her wallet — and now I owe him several hours' worth of baby-sitting. "So I'm forgiven?" I ask hopefully.

"Yes. But don't do it again."

I smile back at him, relieved. That wasn't as bad as I'd thought. I spent all last night worrying about what he'd say to me. I didn't sleep a wink.

"Seth, what's taking you so long?" Polly calls.

He sighs. "Do you mind? She doesn't get many visitors."

I wonder what he means, visitors? "Sure," I say. I guess I'm about to find out.

I step into the hall. It's amazing. The whole

left-hand side is covered in ornate gold frames of different shapes and sizes. Inside the frames are all kinds of things — a glittering paper collage of a rainbow, black-and-white photographs, tiny watercolor landscapes, an oil painting of a shiny red apple — all set against the wine-red wall. It looks incredible, like something out of an interior design magazine.

"Welcome to Polly's Gallery," Seth says, waving his hand at the frames.

I study this amazing black-and-white photograph of a baby. It really draws you in. The baby's eyes are dark, almost black, and staring into them, I can see my own eyes reflected, or maybe it's just a trick of the light.

"She took that when I was ten months old," Seth says softly. "When we were still living in London."

"You lived in London?"

"Until I was one. I don't remember it."

I look at the photo again and smile. "You were a cute baby. And it's a brilliant photo. I can't believe your mum took it."

Seth shrugs. "She was a photographer — sorry, *is* a photographer. But she hasn't worked for a while."

"Seth," his mum calls from the room at the end of the hall.

"Coming, Pol." He rolls his eyes again. "She's so

impatient. And there's something else you should know. She's sick."

"You told me. A virus."

"Oh, I should—"

"Seth!" It seems his mum is getting even more impatient.

He leads me into a room at the back of the flat. It's white and there's a houseplant in every corner. They tower toward the ceiling, their lush green leaves waxy and exotic.

On the right-hand wall, there's a tiled fireplace with a mirror hanging over it. The grate is crammed with lit white candles, and Billy's snoozing in his basket just in front of it. He raises his head, looking at me for a second before going back to sleep.

"I took Billy for a long run on the beach earlier," Seth says. "He's exhausted."

I laugh. "I won't take it personally."

Then I notice a woman lying on a battered leather sofa, surrounded by an army of pillows and cushions.

My eyes take in her pale, thin face—the only color two flushed spots on her cheeks, round and symmetrical like a doll's blush—her unusual navy-blue eyes, the jaunty red pirate scarf on her head, her warm welcoming smile. She's wearing old, paint-splattered jeans and a fluffy white fleece pullover that swamps her small frame. Her bare blue-veined feet are lit up by the fire-engine red of her toenails.

"Hi," she says, beckoning me over. "I'm Polly, Seth's mum. And you are . . . ?"

"This is Amy," Seth cuts in. "A friend from school."

"Sit down." Polly swings her feet onto the floor and pats the sofa to her right. I sit down gingerly, feeling a bit awkward. She looks so tiny and breakable. I know I'm staring at her, but I can't help it. She holds my gaze steadily, and there's steel in her eyes. She reminds me suddenly of Clover, small yet strong.

"Have you offered your guest a drink, Seth?" she says, still looking at me.

"No," he says. "Give me a chance."

"What would you like?" she asks me.

"Nothing, thanks. I'm fine."

"I'd love a tea if you're offering." Polly smiles up at Seth, who is standing just behind her, his hands holding the back of the sofa.

He gives a laugh. "More? You'll drown in the stuff one of these days."

She leans her head back and rubs it against his hands. Her scarf shifts a little, and I see downy blond tufts where her hair should be, like the feathers of a newborn chick or a dandelion clock. I look away quickly.

"He's a good lad," Polly says as soon as Seth's out of the room. "I don't know what I'd do without him." She pulls the scarf back over her forehead, covering her fluff. "God, I miss my hair. What a palaver!" She looks at me. "I presume Seth told you about the chemo?"

I shake my head. "Not exactly. He said you had a virus."

"Oh." She blows out her breath in a *whoosh*. "It was a bit more than that, I'm afraid. I had breast cancer. But luckily they caught it in time, and I was given the all-clear a few weeks ago. It's been a difficult time for both of us. He doesn't like talking about it." She folds her hands in her lap and plays with a chunky silver ring, twisting it around and around her finger. "Sorry, you don't need to know all this. Ignore me."

"No, it's fine. My granny died of breast cancer." Then I realize what I've just said. "But she was much, much older than you," I add quickly. "She was fifty-five."

"I'm thirty-one. If I make it to fifty-five, I'll be a happy woman." She gives me a lovely smile, so warm it's like being bathed in sunlight. "You must miss her." She reaches out and takes my hand. It's cool but not cold, and she has a surprisingly firm grip. She squeezes it gently and then lets go just as Seth walks in the door carrying a small wooden tray.

He puts it on the coffee table and kneels down beside it, pouring Polly a cup of fragrant tea from the flowery teapot. As well as the mug and the teapot, there's a blue bowl on the tray with chocolates in it and a small glass tumbler with a single white sweet-pea flower.

"Yum, peppermint," Polly says as Seth hands her the mug and she sniffs it. She cups her hands around it. "My favorite. So what are the pair of you up to today? Anything exciting?"

For some reason I think of Seth's lips pressing against mine. I blush furiously and look away, pretending to study one of the ferns.

"Nothing special," Seth says. "I was thinking of going to the National Gallery. They have a Rothko on loan from Chicago for a few months. Might be worth seeing. Do you want to tag along, Amy?"

I say, "Cool. I like Rothko."

"Oh, yeah, there's one on your Bebo page, isn't there?"

I nod and smile. I haven't been to the gallery on my own before. I used to go with Dad, but he's too busy these days. It would be an adventure, and as it's kind of educational, Mum would hardly mind.

"That sounds lovely," Polly says. "Wish I had the energy to go with you. Will you bring me back a postcard? Something cheery. A Georgia O'Keeffe flower."

"Amy likes her too," Seth says.

My heart skips a little; he remembers.

"She has good taste," Polly says, smiling at me.

Seth says, "See you later, Pol." Then he walks behind the sofa, bends down, and kisses the top of her head. It's so sweet, so natural, it almost brings tears to my eyes. I can't remember the last time I kissed Mum.

"I'm sorry about your mum," I say as we walk toward the train station.

"She's OK now," he says, but there's a snappy edge to his voice, defiant. "She's better."

I've said the wrong thing. I should learn to keep my mouth shut. "I know. She told me. I was just . . . I just wanted to say something. About your mum . . . you know . . . and the cancer. Sorry . . ." I trail off lamely. I've made a right mess of that.

He doesn't say anything, so to fill the silence I say, "It must have been hard on you. That's all."

"You know the worst thing?" he says after a long

pause. "Seeing her so tired all the time, so sick. She's usually so hyper. That was pretty scary, thinking she might not make it. There's only the two of us. Dad left when I was a baby." He stops walking and looks at me, his eyes dark and intense. "Amy, this is just between us, OK? All of it."

"Of course. You can trust me." *Hug me,* I tell him with my eyes. *Hold me, kiss me.* But he just nods and continues walking.

The Rothko is amazing. A lot of his paintings are kind of depressing, brooding black and bloodred boxes floating on top of each other, flat stone-colored expanses like arctic landscapes.

But the Rothko painting from Chicago isn't at all depressing. It's positively sunny. *Saffron* it's called, a big burst of tangerine orange with a slash of gold through it, so bright you'd swear there was a light behind it, shining through the center.

Seth sits on the wooden bench in front of the painting, staring at it, running his eyes over different parts of its surface, as if he's trying to memorize it. He's lost in the painting, breathing in the oil paint, lapping up the colors, connecting with it. He really is quite something. He is a bit strange, different, but in a nice way. He shifts over on the bench, rests his shoulder against mine, and holds my hand. My heart skips.

"How does it make you feel?" he asks in a low voice. "The painting, I mean."

"Happy," I say. "Alive." He just squeezes my hand and nods, his lips pressed together. Like his mum, he has a firm grip. His eyes are glistening, and I worry that he might be upset, but he gives me a small reassuring smile. I squeeze back.

Chapter 20

I want to tell someone about Seth, about the amazing day we had at the art gallery. About Polly. About holding his hand. About kissing him on the lips.

It all happened very quickly. We were just outside my house; Mum or Dave could have been staring out the window. But I swear I could feel a spark when our lips touched. I'm too shy to tell Clover. She has so much experience with boys — it might sound childish. And she'd be sure to ask embarrassing questions about the kissing part. I want to tell Mills. She'd understand and she'd be so psyched for me, but I can't.

I miss Mills. Really, really miss her. It's like someone's cut off my right arm. I miss chatting with her on the phone; sometimes I pick up my mobile to text or ring her, and then I remember. She doesn't want anything to do with me. She's made that quite clear. Worst of all, the end-of-term party is at Sophie's house in Foxrock. In three weeks. The whole year is invited — it's traditional — so she'll have to let me in. I'm not looking forward to it. But Seth wants to go, so I'm going too.

Until then, I'm supposed to be studying for my end-of-term exams. They start the week after next and finish the day before the party. But, of course, there are distractions. Like Seth. And Clover.

"Mum," I say, "I'm going to Gramps's house. It's way too noisy here. I have to study geography."

Mum looks up from feeding Alex. "Oh, OK. What time will you — oh, Alex!"

She wipes chewed carrot off her cheek. It leaves a slimy line on her skin, like an orange snail's trail. She scowls at him. "Bad Alex."

He just giggles and kicks his feet, delighted with himself.

"Six," I say, getting out of the kitchen before I'm asked to do anything. "I'll be back for dinner."

"Right, Beanie." Clover strides into Gramps's spare room. He's such a sweetie: he's set up a study desk for me with an old Anglepoise lamp on it and one of those office chairs that whooshes up and down when you press a lever. It's cool fun. I've been playing with it while I'm supposed to be learning about rivers and lakes.

"What?" I scowl at her. "I'm supposed to be studying."

She ignores me and plonks her laptop on top of my open geography textbook. She points at the screen. "Look!"

I read the Bebo site out loud. "'I'd like to announce that I'm coming out. Yes, it's true. I'm a lesbian. I'm sure you've already guessed.'" I look up at Clover. "Do you know this girl?" I read her name. "Alanna?"

"No. She e-mailed the agony aunt page. And she's not a lesbian either! She has a boyfriend. But some genius used her password and changed her Bebo site behind her back. This is only a copy. She's taken her page down. She says the lesbian thing was there for two whole days before she saw it. The whole school's talking about it. Luckily her boyfriend seems like a decent guy; he's sticking by her."

"How did they get the password?" I ask nervously. Mills has my password. The very same thing could happen to me!

"She figures it was one of her friends. But they all deny it. They sound a bit like those girls in the shoe shop from what I can make out. True-blooded D4s. Poor girl doesn't know who to trust."

"That's terrible." I instantly forget all about studying geography. "What are you going to tell her?"

"I'm not sure. It's a difficult one. If she doesn't know who did it . . ." Clover shrugs.

"So she has no Bebo page up at the moment?" I ask.

"Nope."

"But everyone's probably checking for her page every day. They'll be wondering what happened, wondering why she doesn't deny it. She should post, pronto, say it was all a sick joke."

"Alanna thinks that would only make everything worse. And she doesn't want to offend any kids who *are* gay."

"Fair point. But she has to fight back, Clover. She can't just let them get away with it."

Clover smiles. "You sound like me, Beanie. But this one has me stumped. Any ideas?"

"Yes, actually. You could help her create a brand-new Bebo page. The ultimate Bebo page. That might distract people and get them talking about something else."

"I like it, Beans. Inspired. We could find her some famous friends."

"And cool music," I add. "And amazing art-work."

"A page so impressive that everyone will forget the coming-out statement ever existed. And it would totally sicken the girls who stitched her up. Who needs friends like that?" Clover pulls out a pink glittery notebook and gel pen. "So tell me about your ultimate Bebo page, Beanie. Think big!"

I consider this for a moment. "My other half would obviously be Johnny Depp, or if he's a bit busy in Hollywood, Dermot O'Leary. I'd have an original song written especially for *moi* by the Script called 'Dear Amy,' and a voice file by Dermot himself saying how much he adores me. Swoon."

"Interesting. I didn't know you were an O'Leary fan as well as a Depp fan. Good taste, Beans. OK, let's e-mail Alanna and get her wish list. And then we should have a meeting with Brains from work."

"Brains? Why?"

She taps her nose twice. "Wait and see, Beanie."

♥ Chapter 21

We meet Brains in a gourmet burger bar in Dun Laoghaire.

When we walk in, a boy about Clover's age waves at her frantically, stands up, and insists on pulling out the heavy wooden chair for her, making it screech on the floor. He's wearing a yellow cotton jacket over a red Hawaiian shirt. I wonder if he's a bit color-blind.

"Hi, Clover," he says, beaming. He can't take his eyes off her. Definite Crushville. Which means I can stare at him and he doesn't even notice. He has really nice teeth, straight and even. In fact, if he got better glasses — his current ones are black-framed and geeky — and a haircut, he'd actually be quite cute. And he has the most amazing skin, coffee-colored, glowing, and not a spot in sight. Plus Bambi eye-lashes. Wasted on a boy.

"Brains, this is Amy, my niece," Clover says. "She'll be joining us today."

His face drops a little. He's obviously a bit surprised to see me. "No problemo," he says. "Now, what would you ladies like? I'm having the chili burger. I like my food hot, hot, hot." He sings the "hot, hot, hot" like a Latin American salsa singer, and I hear Clover give a little sigh under her breath.

After we order — burger and fries for Clover and Brains, salad and fries for me — Clover gets down to business.

"We need your help," she tells him.

"Always happy to help such a *purdy* lady," he says with a toothy grin. He leaves his mouth open and his teeth clenched, like something from a cartoon. *"Ding,"* he says, and points to his exaggerated smile.

"Give me patience," Clover murmurs, and I try not to laugh.

"I want you to create a very special Bebo skin," she says.

"For you?" he asks, as eager as a puppy.

"No, for a friend of mine. Alanna is her name. Now, this is all top secret. . . ." Clover tells him the full story.

After listening carefully, Brains sits back in his seat. "I have a sis, Ria. She's eleven. I'd kill anyone who hurt her. I understand, *amigo*. It's a beautiful thing you're doing, Clover. I knew you were one special lady." He starts to sing again. "Lady, lady, lady, lady," he croons like Frank Sinatra.

"Two Cokes," the waitress interrupts. "And an orange juice?" She smiles down at him. "Nice voice."

"Thank you, sweetheart," he says in his best deep Elvis voice. "You're too kind." He breaks into "Are You Lonesome Tonight?"

The waitress walks off giggling.

"Dear Lord, spare me," Clover says. "Would you stop flirting with the staff, Brains, and concentrate?"

"Sorry, Clover. I didn't realize you were the jealous type. But you know I only have eyes for you, don't ya?" He wiggles his eyebrows up and down theatrically.

"Don't you dare start singing again," Clover says quickly. She pulls out her notebook and pen. "Now, here are our ideas. We'd like lots of animation. And lots of widgets and quizzes. Fancy stuff, OK?"

"Fancy Schmancy is ma middle name," he says. "Hold on to your hats, gals, I'm the sheriff of Fancy Schmancy town."

Clover gives him a withering look, but I just laugh. I love Brains already — he's crazy but funny.

* * *

A week later Clover sends me an e-mail.

Check out Alanna's new site. It rocks. Hate to say it, but Brains is good. Another mission accomplished. Off to write an article on personalized Bebo skins for mag. Catch u.

Clover XXX

I open Alanna's page and laugh out loud. Clover's right — it diamond rocks! It's called "All about Alanna," and the hazy blue-and-silver skin is like nothing I've ever seen before. The surface shimmers and sparkles, like oil on water. The "Alanna" is hand-drawn, each letter interlaced with tiny dragons, rainbows, and Celtic symbols, sparkling with moving stardust. As I watch, a tiny fairy, more Pussycat Dolls than Tinker Bell, flutters her purple wings, flies off the *A*, blows me a kiss, and says, "Welcome to Alanna's Bebo page. Enjoy the trip. 'Cause it is a trip." Then she laughs and disappears off the page.

I scroll down. Alanna has 19,773 profile views already! In case you're not a Bebo aficionado, that's a hell of a lot of views. Mine has 293, and I thought

I was doing well. Plus 2,257 people have sent Alanna love. And that's truly amazing!

But the best is yet to come. Alanna's other half, her most special Bebo friend in the world, is none other than Gordon D'Arcy — or "My Very Own Mr. Darcy," as she calls him — the Irish rugby hero, ultimate D4 and Crombie idol. Her so-called "friends" are going to wet themselves with jealousy. And seven of the Irish squad, including Brian O'Driscoll, another huge star, are her friends. Many of them have left her a special message. Along with Snow Patrol, *Goss* magazine, and several delicious male teen models, one in the shower, not that you can see anything. I chuckle to myself. Clover!

I click on the first of Alanna's flash box clips.

"Hi, Alanna," an incredibly handsome man says in a wonderfully deep voice like gravel. I give a little scream. It's Gordon D'Arcy! His face is shining, and his chest heaves up and down. From the muck on his shirt, he's obviously just come off the pitch. "Just saying howdy to my favorite Bebo chick. How's tricks, Alanna? Hope you got the tickets to the next match."

The second clip is Snow Patrol. "This song is brand-new," the lead singer, Gary Lightbody, says in his sexy Northern Irish drawl. "Just for Alanna. Enjoy, Alanna." He winks at the camera. "And a shout-out to all the girls in the *Goss* office, especially Saffy and Clover." I squeal again. This is just amazing.

Clover is a genius. I don't know how she's managed it, but this page will go down in Bebo history. It's without a doubt the most fab, rocking page I've ever seen. Alanna will be the coolest girl in school.

And that's not all. On her flash box, there's a video of a *Goss* fashion shoot. As I watch, a tall, dark-haired girl is walking down a catwalk, smiling from ear to ear, like she's just sucked on a helium balloon. Her makeup is fantastic, all peacock-blue sparkling eyes and hot-pink lips.

She sashays up and down in a gorgeous red chiffon dress, flipping the floaty hem with her hand, looking like a million dollars. She turns to the camera, beams, and says, "Clover and Amy, you're the best! I don't know how to thank you."

I collapse back into my chair, shaking my head. Clover really is something.

♥ Chapter 22

Two weeks later, exams are finally over — yeah! I think I've done OK in most subjects, apart from Irish and Spanish. And I hate to say it, but math was easy peasy.

But far more important — it's the end-of-term party and I'm mega-nervous. It's at Sophie's house for a start, and she's completely ignoring me at the moment. I don't really care about that, but Mills is still under her evil sorceress spell. I miss Mills horribly. But at least I have Clover.

I ring her in a panic at eight. The party's supposed to start at eight. "Clover, help! I have nothing to wear to this party. And I'm late already."

"Hey, Beanie." Clover's voice sounds strange, like

she's underwater. I can hear a spitting noise and then she says, "Sorry, I was just brushing my tongue. Hot date tonight. Say that again."

"Lucky Ryan."

"Not exactly. He dumped me." She makes a loud raspberry noise. "He's now going out with a girl in his English class."

"When did this happen?"

"The day we went to the zoo. He'd been a bit off for a while; I should have guessed something was up."

"I thought you were quiet that day. But you never said anything."

"To be honest, I didn't really want to talk about it. Besides, after all your dad's news, you had enough to deal with. Anyway, I'm fine now. I've moved on, as you can see."

She doesn't sound all that fine. I know she liked Ryan a lot more than she let on. But I don't want to upset her just before a date.

"So who's the lucky guy?" I ask.

"Don't get too excited. It's only Brains. I owe him one, remember?"

"But I thought you said he was nuttier than Nutella."

She sighs. "Tell me about it. But a promise is a

promise. I'm wearing my sunglasses in case anyone sees me."

I laugh. "Where are you going?"

"God knows. He says it's a surprise. Probably somewhere dorky like the library or a chess competition. Anyway, what can I do you for?"

"I'm having a wardrobe meltdown. I have this end-of-term party." I groan. "Maybe I'll just stay home."

"Oh, no you won't! Give me ten minutes. I'll grab some gear and be straight over. But I'm a bit stuck for time, so I can't give you the full works. Throw on your black skinny jeans, and I'll concentrate on your upper half."

Clover arrives with an armful of tops: floaty chiffon tunics, cotton tanks in rainbow colors, vintage T-shirts, and silk shirts in funky seventies patterns.

"Where'd you get all these?" I ask, sifting through them before she has a chance to put them down.

"You should see the amount of clobber in the mag's offices. It's like a branch of Topshop. All kinds of things get left behind after photo shoots, and then there are the samples and freebies. Saffy says I can borrow what I like. They all do it. And some are actually mine."

She eyes the bed, which is already cluttered with piles of clothes. All tried on and all discarded. My whole room looks like a bomb's gone off in a clothing factory.

Clover drapes her tops over one end of the bed. "You're not usually so bothered about clothes, Beanie. It must be some party." She looks at me and then smiles. "Is it a boy? Is there someone you fancy?"

"No!" I busily flick through the tops. I hold an emerald-green shirt up against my chest and look in the mirror. I wince. I look washed out; the color's far too strong for me. Instead I pick up a fitted red cotton top with tiny pearl buttons down the front.

But Clover's like a dog with a bone. "So who is he? Is it Seth?" As soon as she says his name, my skin prickles and I get that funny feeling in the pit of my stomach.

I spin around. "How do you know about Seth? Have you been spying on me?"

She just grins. "Keep your knickers on, Beans. Sylvie said a Cure Head called Seth's been coming around, that's all. Actually, I think she quite likes him. She says he's brilliant with the little ones."

Great, so now Mum's telling everyone about my private life. Typical! "What's a Cure Head?"

"That's what ancients like Sylvie call goths and

emos. In Sylvie's day, Cure Heads wore black lipstick and white makeup. And they worshiped a band called the Cure."

"I've of heard them. Eighties band, right? 'Lovecats.'"

She nods. "Cute lead singer. Used to live in Killiney."

"Really?"

"Yep. I saw him once in Supervalu."

"You're making that up."

"On Johnny Depp's life," she says, crossing herself. "So go on, tell me about Seth. Does he really wear makeup?"

"Of course not. Just a bit of eyeliner."

"Eyeliner? Hey, that reminds me. Hang on a sec." She runs out the door.

"Clover! You're supposed to be helping me." I put down the red top; it's far too big. It would flap around on me like a circus tent. Instead I find a cool black T-shirt with a woman's head on it; she looks a bit like Marilyn Monroe, bleached blond hair and pouty red lips.

The black material is so faded it's almost green. The name BLONDIE is splashed across the front in red glittery writing that matches the woman's cracked-with-age lipstick. Most of the glitter has worn off, but that only makes it look even more authentic. I hold it up against me and smile. I think Seth will like it; it's perfect.

"Are you ready, Amy?" Mum says up the stairs in her trying-not-to-wake-the-baby voice, a louder and huskier version of a whisper.

"Nearly. Give me two minutes."

"Hurry up. Dave has to get to work. He's going to drop you on the way."

I pull the T-shirt over my head, carefully so I don't smudge my makeup, and then rearrange my hair.

Clover comes back in with a faded blue photo album in her hands.

She looks me up and down. "Not bad. You look like a rocker chick."

I take this as a compliment.

"Nip it in at the waist." She hands me a red leather belt. While I put it on, she flicks through the album, dislodging some of the old photos from their sticky pages, and then says, "Aha." She points at a page. "There you go."

I study the photograph. A teenage boy stares back at me. He looks familiar, but I can't quite place him. "Who's that?"

"Your dad," she says.

"No!" I stare at the picture, and it seems to

rearrange itself right in front of my eyes. She's right. The boy has Dad's soft gray eyes, emphasized by thick kohl eyeliner; his slim nose, complete with the tiny bump from falling off his bike when he was eight; his full lips, painted black in this photograph. He's wearing what looks like a dinner jacket teamed with a white shirt with flouncy ruffles down the front. I hate to admit it, but he's quite good-looking, even in the Dracula outfit.

I give a snort. "Unbelievable."

"Amy!" Mum hisses up the stairs.

"I'm coming, I'm coming."

Clover says, "I'd drive you to the party, Beanie, but I'm kind of late myself." She blows out her breath. "I wish I didn't have to go. Hey, I could always cancel, say I have to take you somewhere urgently."

"Don't use me as an excuse. Be nice to Brains. Please? We do owe him, big-time. Alanna's skin was something else."

She shrugs. "You're right. Fair's fair."

"You never know; he might even grow on you."

"Yeah, right. So not going to happen. I hope this Seth is a bit more exciting than Brain-box. Hey, is he a good snog?"

"Clover!" I can feel my cheeks go red. I knew she'd do this.

193 ♥

She grins. "Only asking."

I busy myself brushing my hair and checking my makeup in the full-length mirror, hoping she doesn't notice how nervous I am.

"Beanie?" Clover says, standing just behind me. She's so close I can feel her warm breath on the back of my neck. She puts her hands on my shoulders and whips me around to face her. She smells of spearmint mixed with musky perfume. "You've kissed a boy before, right?"

I twist my head, avoiding her gaze.

"I'm not teasing you," she says. "I just want to help."

I sigh. I guess I could do with some advice. And Clover does have acres of experience with boys. "Not really," I admit finally.

"I thought as much. It's nothing to worry about. It's all very natural." Her hands rest gently on my shoulders. "First you just gaze into his eyes, like this." I try not to laugh as Clover eyeballs me, her expression soft and kind. "OK, now drop your gaze ever so slightly, as if you're shy. Boys don't like it when you come on too strong at the beginning. They like to think they're in control. Ha! As if. Then you lean in toward —"

"Amy!" Mum appears at the door. "What *are* you doing?" She stares at us. I jump away from Clover, feeling horribly guilty. *Please don't tell her,* I beg silently.

But Clover's no fool. "I was checking Beanie's teeth for lipstick."

"Oh, right. If you want a lift, Amy, you'll have to come right now. Dave's in the car with the engine running. You're going to make him late for work."

"But, Mum, Clover hasn't finished —"

Mum puts her hands on her hips. "No buts, young lady. Now!" She looks very stern.

"Bye, Clover," I say, grabbing my lip gloss, my mobile, and my keys and shoving them in my pockets. "Thanks for all the help."

She winks at me. "Good luck. Ring me tomorrow. And you look great, Beanie. Knock 'em dead."

"You'll need a jacket," Mum says, staring at my bare arms.

"It's a party," I say. "We'll be inside." What is it with mums and jackets? They're obsessed.

"And where on earth did you get that Blondie T-shirt? I had one just like it. But mine went missing years ago."

"Oops," Clover says. "Sorry, Sylvie."

♥ Chapter 23

I make Dave drop me down the road from Sophie's; he's in a hurry, so he doesn't mind.

"Have a nice night," he says through his open window. "Behave yourself. Back before eleven or —"

"Or I'll turn into a pumpkin. I know, I know. But even Cinderella got till midnight, not eleven."

"Don't push your luck. How are you getting home?"

"I'm getting a lift with Mills."

"Good. See you tomorrow." With that, he drives off.

Great, he's swallowed it. I have no intention of getting a lift with Mills. She's not even speaking to me. I plan on grabbing a lift of sorts on Seth's cross-bar, and I don't think Dave would approve.

As I walk down the road toward Sophie's house, my stomach is fluttering butterflies and my palms are hot and sticky. I hate walking into parties on my own. Mills and I have been going to parties together since we were nippers, and I feel naked without her by my side. But then I hear a voice to my right.

"Hi, stranger." I look over. Seth is sitting on the wall outside Sophie's house. His bike is resting against it, and his long legs are dangling over it. He jumps down, catches a pedal with the end of his jeans, and almost sends his bike toppling. I grab it and rest it against the wall again.

"Are you OK?" I ask.

He nods. "Think so." He rubs his ankle. "Sorry, that was stupid." He smiles and I feel all melty inside, like ice cream on a hot day. "Like the T-shirt," he says.

"Thanks, it's vintage." I don't tell him it's Mum's — that would spoil the effect; he's met Mum and he knows how deeply untrendy she is. Now, if I had a mum like Polly, that would be different.

"Polly loves Blondie," he says. "She's always singing 'Call Me' in the shower. Ready for the dragon's den?"

Seth locks his bike against a cherry tree in the

front yard with two other bikes. I'm sure Mrs. Piggott, Sophie's mum, won't be amused to find her tree is being used as a bike rack, but, you know, she's such an old boot that I really don't care. Especially after she said such horrible things about my mum.

Seth reaches out to hold my hand, but I step away a little, pretending I haven't seen it. Walking into the party is going to be hard enough without drawing extra attention to ourselves. Everyone at school knows we're together by this stage — they'd have to be blind not to — but I'm still a bit embarrassed by it all. Sophie and Mills snigger when we walk past them together in school, so I try to avoid the science area completely if at all possible.

"Would you look who it is?" Sophie is framed in the doorway, her hands on her hips. She's wearing tiny denim shorts, new sand Uggs, and an emerald-green Juicy hoodie, with a silver filigree pattern over the shoulders and the arms, zipped up to her neck. I have to admit, she looks lovely, even if her legs are a bit orange. Mills is standing behind her, peering over her left shoulder.

"Our old pal, Amy," Sophie says. "Should we let her in, Mills? What do you think?"

Mills refuses to catch my eye, staring at Seth intently.

"Stop messing around, Sophie," he says evenly. "Here, these are for you. For having the party." He thrusts a gold box of chocolates into her hands. "Pol — my mum insisted."

This throws Sophie a little. "Thanks," she says automatically, looking at me. "But you still can't come in. You're not invited."

I feel instantly flattened and mortified. I can feel my cheeks start to burn. I look at Seth, but he's not budging off the doorstep.

"You can't do that, Sophie," he says coolly. "It's the end-of-term party. Everyone's invited."

"You can come in, Seth," she says. "But Amy can't."

Then I hear a familiar voice. "What's happening?" Annabelle asks, poking her head out the door.

She looks at me and her face drops. "Oh," she says. "You."

Surprisingly, the Dundrum doggy story never reached school. I heard she took Nina and several other friends to a Beyoncé concert in a white limo (her dad is some sort of bigwig in the sales department of a newspaper), and I did wonder whether it was a bribe, designed to keep their mouths firmly shut.

"Let her in," Annabelle says, giving me a very fake smile.

"What?" Sophie says. "Are you serious? Amy's — "

"Just let her in, all right?" Annabelle says, giving Sophie a filthy look. "It's the end-of-term party."

"That's what I told her," Seth says.

Annabelle glares at him. "Don't push it, Ladyboy."

"Who are you calling Ladyboy?" Seth's eyes are flashing.

"If you must wear *guy*liner," Annabelle says, "deal with it."

"Hey," Seth says, moving toward her.

I put my arm out to stop him. "Let's just go inside."

He nods. "Fine."

The stupid thing is I only wanted to go to the party to be with Seth. We should have just gone to the movies or something and told our parents we were at the party. I don't know why I didn't think of it. Too late now.

We walk into the living room, and it's crammed with D4s doing their neat, prissy dancing. The Crombie boys are hanging around the sides of the room, pushing and thumping each other and laughing.

I say hi to some of the girls from my class who are comparing outfits by the French doors. Seth nods at a few emos from art class.

"Outside?" he suggests, pointing at the open doors. I follow him into the garden. There are round red and orange fairy lights threaded through the trees, and a row of paper lanterns lit with tea lights twinkle along the path. A silver wind chime dangles off a lower branch of the big oak tree, making a noise like running water in the breeze. I have to admit the whole garden looks amazing, like a Chinese Wonderland.

We sit down with our backs against the tree, the party babbling away behind us, hidden by the knotty trunk.

"What are we doing here?" Seth asks, banging his head gently against the wood.

I laugh. "I was just thinking exactly the same thing."

He takes my hand, straightens it out, and starts to touch my palm with his fingertips, making me jump. It's like ants running on my skin.

"That tickles," I say, trying to pull my hand away.

He holds firm. "You have a very long lifeline," he says, running his forefinger firmly down the center of my palm. "Deep and true. That's a good sign. And this is your happiness line, right here." He strokes the top of my palm. "Again, strong but a little broken and hatched at the start."

"That would be my parents' divorce, then," I say wryly. "Do you really read palms, or are you making this up?"

"My mum does, so I've picked up a bit. She's really good at it. I'll get her to give you a proper reading one day."

"Cool." But I like the sensation of *his* skin against mine, so I say, "Keep going. What else can you see?"

"Your palm is rectangular, which means you have a strong imagination and you dream a lot. Like mine, see?" He holds up his own hand and marks out a rectangle with his finger. He's right. Our hands are quite similar in shape.

"Go on," I say.

"You see the small horizontal lines there?" He presses gently on the fleshy part of my palm, just under my thumb.

"Yes?"

"They mean you like to enjoy yourself, but you also have a serious side, which can sometimes be hidden."

"That's true!" I give a laugh.

He closes my fingers over my palm. "That's all I remember."

"I'm impressed. Not just a pretty face, Ladyboy."

He grins. "Hey, less of that." He stops for a

moment, then says, "You don't mind the eyeliner, do you?"

"Not at all. I like it. It makes you different. Original."

Seth goes quiet for a second. He's staring at me.

"What?" I ask, a little paranoid. Have I said the wrong thing?

"I really like you, Amy." His face moves a little closer, and my heart almost leaps out of my chest with fright. OK, OK, this is it. Crunch time. Now what did Clover say again? Lean toward him. OK, I'm doing that. Catch his eye, then look down a little, then back up and . . .

His lips meet mine, and there it is again, instant electricity. This time neither of us moves away. But I have no idea what to do next. *Help!* I think as his lips press against mine, gentle yet firm. What am I supposed to do now? Clover didn't get this far. His hand is resting against the back of my head now, pulling against my hair. It's not very comfortable, but I try to ignore it. I move my lips against his (it seems the right thing to do), but then I feel the tip of his tongue against my lower lip. I open my own lips a little, and — *CLINK* — my teeth crunch against his. I jump back in fright.

"Sorry, Amy," he whispers.

Meltdown. I'm mortified. "It's fine," I mumble. "Loo. Stay there. Back in a sec."

I run inside cringing. *Loo? What age are you, Amy? Three?* I walk quickly through the living room, looking straight ahead, oblivious of the people around me, and out into the hall. I have to be alone, at least until my cheeks have stopped burning and I can face Seth again. But there's someone in the downstairs toilet. I run upstairs instead, past Sophie's room, and into the huge marble bathroom. I slam the door behind me and sit down on the closed loo seat.

I think about ringing Clover, but what would I say? I clashed teeth with Seth — what do I do now? Even Clover would laugh. No, I'll have to think of some other way to get the information out of her.

Ten minutes later, I'm starting to feel better. Seth has texted me. SO SORRY. ALL MY FAULT. STILL UNDER THE TREE. R U OK? I look in the mirror. My cheeks are almost back to normal, so I open the door and step out.

"Young lady?"

I swing around. Mrs. Piggott is staring at me.

"Amy! What are you doing up here?"

"Using the loo. The one downstairs was busy."

"I see." From the suspicious look on her face, I can tell she doesn't believe me.

"How's your mum?" she asks.

"Fine, thanks." I so want to add, "And you'll be delighted to hear she's not having any more babies either," but I don't dare. Mrs. Piggott is scary. She's wearing a white high-collared Victorian-looking shirt tucked into ultra-dark jeans with iron creases down the front. They're Rock & Republic, which I know cost a fortune (Clover has a pair she got in a sale), but they just look wrong on someone her age. And they look plain daft with her pink fluffy slippers. As usual, her face is caked with thick orange makeup. I can see where Sophie gets her sense of "style."

"Good. Now, run along, Amy dear — downstairs, please. No one's allowed up here."

"Sorry, sorry," I say completely tongue-tied. She always makes me feel so horribly guilty.

In the living room, Annabelle and Nina are setting up a game of spin the bottle. Nina clicks her chicken-bone fingers at Sophie. "Get us another bottle, will you? A glass one if you have it. This one doesn't spin properly."

Sophie comes back in with a full wine bottle. She hands it over to Nina. "This is the only glass one I could find."

Nina grins. "Good for you, Soph. I love white wine, and it's screw top too, even better."

"You can't drink it," Sophie stammers. "It's just for the game."

Nina just winks at her. *Oops*, I think, *Sophie's in for trouble.*

I catch Mills's eye, and we stare at each other. Almost automatically I raise my hand and give her a small wave. She doesn't wave back, but her lips lift a little and she rolls her eyes to heaven in true Mills style, as if to say, "Spin the bottle, how lame is that?" But then Sophie says something to her and she gets distracted.

I want to talk to Mills, to tell her I miss her, but not in the middle of a party, in front of all the D4s. If she rejected me in front of them, I think I'd shrivel up and die on the spot. But she did smile at me, so maybe there's a glimmer of hope.

As I walk back toward the tree, my nerves are jangling under my skin, like a bad case of pins and needles. But when I approach, Seth just smiles up at me in an easy way and pats the grass beside him.

"Long time no see," he says.

"They're playing spin the bottle inside," I say without thinking. Then I cringe.

He laughs. "Can you imagine having to kiss Sophie or Annabelle?" He pulls a face. "Grim! I'd say they'd eat you alive." Then he realizes what he's just said, but we both choose to ignore it.

I sit down beside him, and he wiggles in toward me so our sides are meshed together like Siamese twins. He takes my hand and envelops it in both of his. I feel warm and protected.

"Have you talked to Mills yet?" he asks.

"No. But she rolled her eyes at me just now."

He laughs again. "Is that a good or a bad sign?"

"Good, I think."

"You must miss her."

"Yeah. But what can you do?" I sigh.

He squeezes my hand, and I rest my head on his shoulder.

"Let's split," he says. "Leave them all to it. I'm only here 'cause I wanted to see you."

"Me too."

Seth walks me home. It's miles away and it takes two hours, but we're in no hurry. We chat and laugh the whole time. Seth and I, we just click. It's so easy being around him; there's no pretending. I can just be myself.

He kisses me outside my door. And this time both our mouths stay firmly shut just in case. But before I pull away, I run the tip of my tongue along his top lip. I don't know what possesses me, but it's done before I can stop myself; he's just so delicious. He smiles and then kisses both my eyelids, making my heart flutter.

"Can I see you tomorrow, Amy?"

I nod and grin.

♥ Chapter 24

To: agonyaunt@gossmagazine.com
Sunday

Dear Clover,

I really like this guy, and I think he likes me too. Last weekend at a party, we kissed for the first time. It was terrible—our teeth clashed, and then we both pretended it had never happened. I'm morto. Am I horribly abnormal?

Was I doing it all wrong? Can you give me some tips on how to kiss? Properly, I mean. I'd be so grateful.

From Samantha, 14, in Dundalk

P.S. If you don't want to answer my letter on your agony aunt page, maybe you could reply to me privately, or if you don't have the time, how about an article on kissing. You could call it "Kissing with Confidence."

I click on SEND. I know setting up a fake e-mail address is kind of sneaky, but I'm too embarrassed to ask Clover directly. This way I hope I'll get the information I desperately need, and fast!

When I get home on Sunday, Mum is in my room, practically naked. She's standing in front of my mirror in her red-and-white-checked bikini. She's holding a fold of tummy skin in one hand and pushing up her breasts with the other.

"What on earth are you doing?" I ask.

She gives a shriek. "Amy, you nearly gave me a heart attack." Her cheeks and chest are burning, and there are still red marks on the pale skin of her stomach where her hands have been. She whips her head around, looking for something to cover her up. I hand her a T-shirt.

"Thanks," she says, pulling it over her head. It just about fits. She still looks very flustered. "If you must know, I was trying on my bikini. But I think my bikini days are over." She gives a long, drawn-out sigh. "Don't have children, Amy. It ruins your figure."

"Mum, I'm thirteen! I'm not exactly planning on it any time soon."

"Of course not, sorry. It's just all a bit depressing. I used to have such lovely boobs, and now they're heading south. If I wasn't so scared of hospitals, I'd probably have a tummy tuck."

"Surgery?" I sit down on my bed and stare at her. "Isn't that a bit extreme?"

She shrugs. "There's this wobbly bit that I can't seem to shift." She lifts up the T-shirt and grabs her stomach again. She's right, but I know when to keep my mouth shut.

"You look great in your new clothes," I say. The president herself would be proud of my diplomacy. "That's what matters. And you can always wear a tank-ini instead."

"A tankini?"

"You know, like a bikini but with a tank top that covers your stomach. They're cool. Clover has one."

"If Clover has one, they must be way cool," Mum snaps. "Not that she needs to hide her stomach."

"I'm only trying to help."

"I'm sorry, pet. Ignore me. How's Mills?"

"Fine." I was actually at Seth's place, watching a

movie this afternoon, but I told her I was hanging out with Mills. It meant less explaining.

"Good, I'm glad you two are getting along all right. She hasn't been here for a while, and I was beginning to wonder."

"Everything's fine. So stop worrying."

"I'm your mum. That's my job." She ruffles my hair, and I swat her hand away.

Mum hogs the Internet all night, so I don't get a chance to IM Seth, like we'd arranged. At ten he texts me: SLEEP WELL, AMY. SETH X

A kiss, he sent me a kiss. I know it's not a huge deal, but it's the first X he's sent me. I save the message immediately and hold my mobile to my chest. He X's me. Seth X's me!

It's now Wednesday, and I (well, technically "Samantha") still haven't heard back from Clover. What if Seth wants to kiss me? I've been worrying about it all day. When I walk in the door, Dave is standing in the hall, Evie in his arms and Alex clinging on to his legs.

"Can you take Evie?" he says, thrusting her toward me.

"Hang on, I haven't even put my bag down yet,"

I say, slightly miffed. No "Hello, Amy, lovely to see you. How's tricks?" Not in this house.

I dump my bag under the coat hooks. "Where's Mum?"

"In there." He points to the living room. "She's playing with her new toy. It was delivered this morning. But don't open the—"

It's too late. I push the door, and Alex darts in. He's faster than a jaguar.

Dave says, "Grab him!" and I run after him but stop dead in amazement when I see Mum. She's pounding away on a huge running machine. Her cheeks are deep tomato red, and her forehead is glistening.

Alex is trying to get up on the treadmill behind her. I grab his waist and swing him away.

"No you don't, buster," I say. "That's dangerous." He squeals and kicks my shins. His heels are surprisingly sharp.

"Thanks," Mum says breathlessly. "Can't stop. Have to finish my miles."

I'm impressed. "How many miles have you done?" I ask her.

"Nearly one."

It doesn't sound like much, but I don't want to discourage her. "It looks fun. Can I have a go later?"

"It's not a toy, Amy." She winces. "Ow, ow, ow, my side, I've got a stitch. Aagh!" She stops running, and the treadmill powers her backward and spits her off the end. She falls in a heap, her bottom landing with quite a thump on the wooden floor.

I wince. Poor Mum.

"Are you OK, Sylvie?" Dave asks from the doorway.

"No, I'm not OK." She puffs and pants for a few seconds and then says, "I was fine until Alex and Amy distracted me"— more puffing and panting —"I asked you to do one simple thing for me, Dave"— puff, puff —"to keep Alex out of my hair for half an hour." Puff, puff. "I'll never get my figure back at this rate. Aagh!" She gives such a loud groan that Evie starts to howl.

Dave says in a slightly clipped voice, "I'll just take Evie for her walk. Amy, can you play with Alex in the backyard so your mum can finish her marathon running?"

"It's too late now," Mum says, using the sofa to get up. She pushes her sweaty hair back off her forehead. "I'm going to have a shower." She hobbles out of the room, her body bent in two like a pretzel.

Dave shakes his head. "I don't know why she's so

obsessed with getting her figure back. She's fine the way she is."

"Maybe you should try telling her that," I say.

He looks at me in surprise. "Maybe you're right." Evie gives an almighty squawk, like a parrot. "But first I'd better walk this madam."

Thursday and still not a peep from Clover. I decide to ring her.

"Hi, Beanie," she says. "I'm sorry I haven't rung. It's been crazy all week. I've been helping out on the summer fashion spreads. Running around the shops and collecting clothes, assisting the photographer — he's pretty cute too; has a model girlfriend, though, bummer."

"How was your date with Brains?"

Silence for a moment.

"Clover, are you still there?"

"Actually he's kind of growing on me," she admits eventually.

"I told you."

"Yeah, yeah, you were right. Stop gloating. We went to this karaoke bar with some of his mates from the band. It was hilarious. And he's a brilliant singer."

"He's in a band?"

"Yep, the Golden Lions. They're kind of indie but with a sixties edge. Lots of jingly guitars and poppy bits. He's going to write a song for me."

"Swoon. A rock-star boyfriend. Clover, you're so lucky."

She tells me more about her date, and when I click my mobile off, I realize I've forgotten to ask her about work. And most important, about any letters she may have received. *Siúcra*, as Clover would say!

♥ Chapter 25

"I'm sooo fat," Shelly moans, rubbing her slightly rounded belly.

"Mum's tummy is way bigger than that, and Evie's three months old," I tell her scornfully. The second the words are out of my mouth, I feel disloyal and slightly grubby.

Shelly's eyes go all wide, like an owl's. "You mean I'll be fat forever? How depressing."

"Sylvie's a lot older than you," Dad says. "You'll get your figure back in no time."

This annoys me. Dad's no spring chicken himself, plus he's years older than Mum, so I say, "Actually, you're wrong, Dad. Mum says babies wreck your figure. She's been running miles every day on her new treadmill, but it's not making any difference. She's talking about getting a tummy tuck."

Shelly wails and tears prick her eyes. "You see, Art? I'm going to be fat for the rest of my life. I knew this was a bad idea." She gets up from the kitchen table and runs out of the room.

"You're the one who wanted a baby in the first place," he shouts after her.

"Dad!" I say, shocked. "That's not very nice."

He puts his head in his hands. "Sorry, I know." He looks up. "She's just being impossible at the moment. She's not rational; she cries at *EastEnders* and the ads about the African babies."

I smile. "It's only her hormones. Mum was like that before she had Alex and Evie. It's perfectly normal."

He shakes his head a little. "When did you get so clever, Amy?"

I shrug. "When you weren't looking, I guess."

He grins and gives a laugh. Then he looks at his watch. "I'd better run or I'll be late for golf. Are you sure you're OK with this? I can drop you home if you like."

It's lovely and quiet in Dad's place, and he says I can order Domino's Pizza for lunch and use the Internet all day. Go back to the madhouse or stay here? Hmm, difficult one, even if it does mean avoiding the Secretary. . . .

"I'll be fine here," I say. "You can drop me back after golf. But are you sure I won't be in the way?"

"Of course not. Shelly plans to rest. You won't even see her."

Excellent.

After two hours on the Internet, I get bored and decide to take Justin for a walk around Phoenix Park. Shelly's delighted and tells me to take my time. He tries to run after a deer, but I hold the leash tight. His little legs are still going, like he's riding a bike, but his body stays still. He's hard work but very cute, a bit like a baby, I suppose. He only poops once, and I use a cardboard pooper scooper like a good citizen. It's only fair. I've stepped in enough dog poo in my time to know how annoying and stinky it is.

When I return, there's a funny smell in the hall that makes my nose tickle. I put Justin in the back garden and go inside to investigate. I walk up the stairs and hear music. It's Shelly. She's singing along to an old ABBA song on the radio, badly, while running a yellow paint roller up and down a wall. She's wearing one of Dad's old work shirts, white with a blue pinstripe and splattered with paint, and her hair is scraped back off her face. She looks younger than Clover.

I watch her for a few minutes before she notices me.

"Amy." She gives a nervous smile. "How long have you been standing there?"

I say nothing. I turn away.

"Amy? Amy?" She follows me into the hall. "Where are you going?"

"Somewhere I'm actually wanted."

I run down the stairs, open the front door, and walk straight into Dad.

"Where are you off to?" he asks me in a cheery voice. He must have won his golf game.

"Home," I say flatly.

"What's going on? I said I'd take you back. Where's your bag?" And then he says gently, "Why are you crying?"

"My bag is in my room, or should I say the *baby's* room," I answer, blinking back the tears. I don't want to cry; I just can't help it. "She's painting it yellow. I hate yellow!"

"I don't understand. Who's painting your room?"

"*She* is."

"She's *what*?" Dad's eyes spark and his nostrils

flare, like a pony's. I know it's petty, but I'm delighted to see how annoyed he is. He drops his golf clubs with a clatter on the marble tiles in the hall and runs up the stairs, taking two at a time. I follow closely behind him.

Shelly is standing at the top of the stairs.

"What are you doing, Shelly?" he demands.

She looks very sheepish. "I just thought . . ." She's standing statue-still with the yellow roller in her hand. It starts to drip on the beige carpet in the landing. Dad grabs it off her and thrusts it into the paint tray in what used to be my room.

"This is Amy's room," he says, waving his arms around at the walls. "It will always be Amy's room. End of story. We've discussed this, Shelly. The baby is going to have the attic room."

"This one is nicer," Shelly says. "The light's better, and the attic's miles away from our room."

"But it's Amy's room," he repeats. "We'll talk about this later. Right now I need to take Amy home."

Shelly looks at me and then at Dad. Her bottom lip starts to quiver, and her eyes are hazy with tears. "I'm sorry, Amy," she says, dropping her head. "I'm so sorry. I just want the baby to be happy. And I'm worried I won't hear it cry. You hear all these awful things about crib death."

Dad takes her hand. "Shelly, the baby's going to sleep in with us for the first while. And after that we'll buy the best baby monitor on the market. He doesn't need Amy's room."

"He?" I ask. "Is it a boy?"

Dad says, "If it's not, we're sending it back."

Shelly lets out a wail. "What if it's a girl?"

"Oh, for goodness sake, Shelly," Dad says. "I'm only joking. Come here." He takes both her hands in his and squeezes them. "I'd be delighted with either, honestly. Don't go upsetting yourself over nothing. Amy says it's perfectly normal to feel a bit weepy at the moment. It's your hormones — isn't that right, Amy?"

"Yes. Mum was always crying," I say grudgingly.

"Sylvie hates me." Shelly sniffs.

"What?" I say, surprised. "She doesn't hate you." I want to add, "She should, but she doesn't," but I stop myself.

Shelly is insistent. "Yes, she does. And I don't blame her. She's so capable and so together. She makes me feel like such a ninny."

"Sylvie doesn't hate you," Dad tells her, backing me up. "You heard Amy. Everything's fine."

"Maybe Sylvie doesn't," Shelly says. "But Amy does. She won't even say my name. I have noticed, you know; I'm not stupid. I know I shouldn't have stolen her room like that—I don't know what came over me." She looks at me, her eyes still flooded with tears. "I'm so sorry, Amy. It was just a fit of madness."

"But you bought the paint," I point out calmly. "And you waited until Dad and I were both out of the house." I'm not going to let her get away with it that easily. I'm not stupid either.

"What do you mean?" she asks.

I say, "You obviously had it all planned. But I came back early and ruined it for you."

Then she starts bawling again. She's such a drama queen. "I'm so sorry," she sobs. "I just wanted—"

"You just wanted your own way, Shelly," Dad says curtly. "What's new?"

I look at Dad and then back at Shelly. They both look miserable. Suddenly I start to feel a bit sorry for her. She's all over the place at the moment, and for a total control freak that can't be much fun. And Dad can be quite sharp with her sometimes. Unlike Mum, who always fought back, Shelly just seems to take it.

What is it about this family? Can't anyone be happy?

Then suddenly I remember what Clover said about being the bigger person. I visualize the attic. It's actually a really big space, with two roof windows and its own bathroom. Then I surprise myself by saying, "You know, Dad, maybe she's right. The baby should be near you. I like the attic. There's more room up there, and if you put in a telly and a sofa, it would make a cool den."

Dad stares at me. "Are you sure, Amy? You don't have to decide now."

I shrug. "It's only a room. The baby's more important than a room."

"Amy Green," Dad gushes, "what a lovely thing to say. I'm so proud of you." He puts his arms around me, but I shrug them off.

"Dad, get a grip." Not him as well.

Shelly wipes away her tears and looks at me. "Thanks, Amy. I really am sorry." She's holding her stomach protectively.

I look back at her. I just nod. My own stomach doesn't feel clenched and anxious like it usually does when I talk to her. It feels, well, normal. I realize now she's just trying to do her best, even if she is the most selfish and annoying woman on the planet. I also realize she's a bit under Dad's thumb. Why is everything always so complicated?

And you know something? Being civil to Shelly doesn't feel all that bad. It's a lot easier than being nasty to her. Let's get this straight: I don't like her or anything, but I don't hate her, either. It's far too exhausting. I've been blaming Shelly for my parents' breakup for four years. It's hard to let go of something like that. But maybe it's time.

And I'm secretly pleased about the attic room. I can watch telly and surf the Net all night, and Dad will never know. And if I ask him now, when I'm Miss Popular in his eyes, he might even buy me my own laptop!

Dad drops me off at the gate. He kisses me on the cheek. "Better get back to Shelly," he says. "Before she paints more of the house behind my back. And thanks again, Amy. I know she can be quite difficult sometimes, but she means well. Thanks for making an effort. I know she's not exactly your favorite person."

I look at him for a moment. "No, I still think Shelly's —" I stop myself. "Look, it doesn't matter. But the baby does matter. I'll get used to her."

He smiles at me.

"What?"

"It's the first time you've used her name."

He's right. I shrug and smile back. "Just a momentary lapse. See ya."

As I walk up the path, Mum swings open the

door. She doesn't look too happy. What now? Dave is standing behind her.

"You're in big trouble, young lady," she says as I walk into the hall. "Antonia rang earlier, and you have some serious explaining to do."

"Who's Antonia?"

"Sophie's mum."

Then the penny drops — Mrs. Piggott must have been spying on me and Seth in the garden. "We were only kissing!" I say quickly. "I swear. Nothing happened."

Mum looks confused. "Kissing? What are you on about? Antonia's pearls are missing. She's says you stole them. Is it true?"

I'm horrified. "Of course not!" I say loudly.

"All right," Mum says. "I hear you, but Antonia is insistent —"

Dave cuts in. "It's best to tell the truth, Amy. If you did take them and you give them back, she says she won't press charges. Otherwise she'll have to report it to the guards."

I stare at him. "I don't believe this. You think I took her pearls, don't you? You believe that old witch."

"Amy!" Mum says.

"I'm sorry, but she's horrible. You should hear what she says about you, Mum."

"Amy," Mum says, "that's quite enough. Of course we don't believe her. Come into the kitchen, and we'll talk about it. Evie's asleep."

In the kitchen, I tell them the whole story, how I had to use the loo, how Mrs. Piggott found me in the hall upstairs.

"But I didn't go near her pearls, Mum, honestly. I didn't even see them."

"She says she had them on the morning of the party, then she changed later that day and put them in the drawer of her dressing table, where she always leaves them. She was quite specific about the details. When she went to look for them this morning, they were gone. She says no one's been near her bedroom since the party."

Dave mutters, "I can believe that, all right."

I snort a laugh, and Mum glares at him. "Dave!"

He says, "Sorry, sorry." But he doesn't look very sorry.

"You're not being very helpful," she tells him.

"I'll just go and check on Alex, then." He walks out of the room in a bit of a huff.

"Look, Amy," says Mum, getting back to business, "this is serious. Antonia claims you're the only person who was upstairs during the party."

"But I was using the loo!" I tell her again.

"She also told me about your fight with Sophie and Mills. Apparently it's been going on for weeks. Is that true?"

"Yes. I suppose so."

"So you weren't at Mills's house yesterday?"

"No. I was at Seth's. And before you say anything — yes, his mum was in. You can ring and ask her if you don't believe me."

"We'll deal with that later. Right now, there are more important things to worry about. Amy, Antonia's very upset. Like Dave said, she's talking about going to the guards. If you tell me you didn't take the pearls, I believe you. But do you understand how serious this is?"

"Yes! Why on earth would I take her pearls? I don't even like pearls. It doesn't make any sense. If I wanted to get back at Sophie, there are plenty of ways I could do that, believe me. And it wouldn't involve stealing her mother's stupid pearls."

Mum shrugs. "You're right. It doesn't make any sense. But she's coming around first thing in the morning so you'd better hide. I don't know what I'm going to tell her."

I feel physically sick. And poor Mum: a visit from Antonia Piggott is the last thing she needs.

"I didn't take them," I say again.

"I know, pet. But somebody at that party did." She pats my hand. "Do you want anything to eat? We've had dinner. There's some roast chicken and potatoes left if you fancy it." Mum's always trying to feed me. Even at odd times like this.

"No, thanks," I say. "I'm not hungry." My stomach is in knots, and I have no appetite. "Mum, if Mrs. Piggott's serious about calling the guards, and they don't believe me, what will happen?"

"Try not to worry about it. You've done nothing wrong. It's all pure speculation at this stage. Maybe the pearls will turn up."

At nine o'clock, I hear a clattering noise on my bedroom window. I look out. It's Mills. She's standing in my back garden, throwing pebbles at the glass. I open it.

"What are you doing?" I whisper loudly.

"I know who took the pearls," she hisses up at me. "I have a plan. Come down. And wear black. Won't be difficult for you. Your wardrobe is full of funeral gear."

I grin. The old Mills is back. Suddenly I start to feel a whole lot better.

♥ Chapter 26

It's late, and Mum and Dave are hardly going to let me out, so I don't even bother asking. I creep down the stairs and past the living-room door, which is slightly ajar. Mum's asleep on the sofa, snoring gently, her feet resting on Dave's lap; Dave's watching a James Bond film with the sound way down, cradling Evie in the crook of his left arm and feeding her a bottle, his eyes glued to the screen.

I sneak into the kitchen and open the back door into the garden. The way I see it, I'm in so much trouble already, it doesn't really matter if I do get caught.

Mills is sitting on the garden bench, waiting. She smiles at me a little shyly. "Hi," she says, standing up but not moving toward me, her hands hanging limply at her sides. She's wearing black jeans, a black cardigan, and cute blue polka-dot flip-flops, which rather ruin the CIA special-agent look.

"Hi," I say back. For a moment we both stare at each other awkwardly.

Then she says, "It was Sophie."

"*What* was Sophie?"

"Sophie took Piggy's pearls." I'd forgotten she'd nicknamed Mrs. Piggott "Piggy."

"Sophie? Are you sure?"

She nods. "She has her own, but she wanted to wear a double string like some celeb or other. So she borrowed her mum's. I don't know why she bothered — you couldn't even see them under her hoodie. I'm the only person who knows she was wearing them. But she lost them in the garden."

For a second I don't know what to say. Then I let rip. "That cow let me take the blame for it! Her mum's threatening to get me arrested. I hate her!"

"I know," Mills says quietly. "And I'm so sorry, about everything. She's not who I thought she was. The only person Sophie Piggott cares about is herself. I should have seen that a long time ago. Can we be friends again, Amy? Please?"

My heart jumps a little, like a stone skimming

on the sea. "Yes!" I want to say. "I've missed you so much."

But I don't. I'm still full of wounded pride. "We'll see," I mumble instead.

"Oh." Mills seems deflated.

"What's your plan, then?" I ask.

"We need to get to Foxrock, and fast. We need evidence. Otherwise it's her word against mine."

"Clover!" we both say simultaneously.

"So explain this to me again," Clover says as we zip toward Foxrock in her Mini. "The pearls are in Sophie's garden somewhere. How big is this garden exactly?"

"Pretty big," Mills admits. "The size of a couple of field-hockey pitches."

"I hope you've brought a sniffer dog," Clover says. "I'm not scrabbling around in stinky cat-pee flower beds."

"I think I know where to start looking," Mills says. "Sophie was snogging Mark Delaney in her garden shed."

"No!" I say. "Really?" I give a snort of laughter. "Clover, remember Annabelle, that girl in the shoe shop?"

"The one who barked for me?"

"Yes."

Mills squeals. "I heard that story. Nina told every-one at the party after she'd drunk Piggy's wine. Anna-belle nearly had a seizure. They had a huge catfight. Was that really you pretending to be a casting agent, Clover?" She gazes at Clover in awe.

"Sure was, honey bun," Clover drawls in her best American accent.

"Mark is only Annabelle's boyfriend," I say, get-ting back to the point.

"The whole gang's falling apart," Mills says. "Nina and Annabelle are at each other's throats. And Anna-belle has cut Sophie off completely. Mark told her Sophie hopped on him."

I laugh again, and then something occurs to me. "Is that why you want to be friends now?" I ask her. "Because your gang is imploding?"

"No!" Mills says. "It's because I miss you, stupid. You're my best friend, and I trust you. You always tell me the truth, even if it hurts sometimes. That's why."

I don't know what to say to that.

A little later we're sneaking around the back of Sophie's house. We've come up with a plan. I hope to goodness it works.

First, Clover makes us all pull black tights over our heads. She says bare skin shines in the dark, and we don't want to get caught. But she doesn't want to wreck good tights, so we leave the legs on and wrap them around our necks like scarves.

"I hope these tights are clean." Mills giggles as she adjusts the gusset over her ponytail.

Clover also has a flashlight, borrowed from Gramps's toolbox under the stairs. She's like Nancy Drew, only way cooler. She's taking this very seriously, right down to Gramps's baggy fishing jacket with huge flappy pockets that are lumpy with spy gear. She's even borrowed his binoculars, although she left them in the car after Mills pointed out she'd need night goggles, not binoculars.

"Keep to the edges, girls," she whispers. "Walk slowly and stay in the shadows. If you hear me whistle like this"—she gives two short blasts—"then back to the car pronto."

"Yes, sir," Mills says, saluting like she's in the army.

I giggle.

"Stop messing, you two," Clover says. "This is serious. We want to get Amy out of the *merde*, don't we?"

"*Absolument*," Mills says firmly.

We creep down the garden toward the shed. Clover glances around furtively and then looks down at the padlock on the door. "I expected as much." She takes a pair of pliers with a long end, like a bird's beak, out of her pocket and starts to poke around in the lock.

Click. It opens.

"Bingo!" she says, sliding the bolt across and pulling open the door. "Follow me, troops." She flicks on her flashlight and shines it around the shed. There are cobwebs in all the corners, and ivy is growing through the roof. I spot an old pink-and-white plastic playhouse and a Barbie bike, still with its training wheels on. They must be Sophie's. Clover shines the flashlight on the floor, its creamy light making sweeping patterns on the rough wood.

"What's that?" Mills asks, pointing at something. There's what looks like a white bead lodged under one of the bike's wheels.

Clover picks it up and rolls it between her finger and thumb. Then she puts it in her mouth and bites down. *Crunch*.

"Bingo!" She grins. "This, my friends, is a pearl. Amy, this is looking good. On your knees, girls. And gloves on. We're going pearl fishing."

We all pull on our thin surgical gloves. Clover uses

them to keep fake tan off her hands. She's thought of everything.

Clover's right. The floor is littered with pearls, and we harvest them, slipping each one into Clover's generous pockets.

Suddenly lights click on outside the house, beaming through the shed's small window. We hear footsteps scrunching down the gravel path.

"Hide!" Clover hisses. She doubles over and dives through the door of the plastic playhouse. Mills follows her.

I crawl behind a rusty green wheelbarrow, my breath ragged and puffy with fright. Seconds later there's a bang on the door, and it swings open.

"I know you're in there," Mrs. Piggott says, her voice quivering but strong. "I've called the guards; they're on their way."

"I have my hockey stick," Sophie shrieks. "And I'm not afraid to use it."

"Pity you're so rubbish at hockey, then," Mills says. She pops her head out of the plastic house and then climbs out. She whips the tights off her head, making her hair go all static. "Hello, Sophie, Mrs. Piggott." She lingers on the "Pig" of Piggott. "I'm sure you're wondering what we're doing in your shed. Clover will explain. Won't you, Clover?"

Clover climbs out of the playhouse and looks at Mrs. Piggott. "My clients have hired me to investigate a wrongful accusation of theft." She straightens her back, making herself taller. "Sorry, I should explain. I'm Clover Hitchcock. Private investigator. I'm actually a lot older than I look."

"No, you're not!" Sophie exclaims. "You're Amy's friend from the Sinister Frite Night."

Clover says smoothly, "I was undercover, working on another case at the time. A very sensitive case to bring down a certain teenage boy who wasn't behaving himself."

Sophie stares at Clover with her mouth hanging open in shock.

Mills adds, "And Clover was the American casting agent in the shoe shop in Dundrum. The one who made Annabelle bark. She's an amazing actress."

Sophie's face is getting whiter and whiter by the second. She looks at her mum. "Don't believe a word they're saying. I have no idea what they're doing in here." She points at me. "But Amy's the thief."

"I am not," I say, glaring at her. "And soon we'll have proof. Show them, Clover."

Clover reaches into her pocket and pulls out a

handful of pearls. She shines her flashlight over them, and they gleam in the light, like tiny birds' eggs. "We found these in this shed," she says.

Mrs. Piggott looks at the pearls. "Are they my pearls? Did you break the cord, you stupid girl?" She glares at me, her eyes narrowing. "Are you trying to plant them here to get out of this?"

How dare she! "No!" I say sharply. "Clover, I'll let you take over."

Clover whips a small plastic bag filled with talcum powder and a paintbrush out of a pocket. She dips a pearl in the powder and then brushes the excess off with the brush. "Just dusting for fingerprints, Mrs. Piggott. We were going to leave this bit to the guards, but seeing as you're both here. . . ." She hands the bag with talcum powder in it to Mills and puts the pearl in a clear plastic sandwich bag.

Then she takes an ink pad out of another pocket and opens it. "I'll need to take some fingerprint samples. You first, Mrs. Piggott, to rule yours out. Then Sophie."

"Why me?" Sophie asks quickly.

"Because you're a suspect," Clover says calmly. "You were spotted in this shed with a certain Mark Del—"

"Stop!" Sophie says.

But it's too late. Mrs. Piggott is staring at her. "You were in here with a *boy*, Sophie?"

Sophie stares down at the floor. "No! She's lying."

"Look at me, young lady. Is that why your neck was all red after the party? Answer me!"

Sophie gives a dramatic sigh. "OK, so I was kissing a boy. Big deal! But it doesn't mean anything, Mum. Amy still took your pearls."

"Sophie," Mills says, shaking her head. "Just tell the truth. Amy doesn't deserve this. It's not fair."

"Oh, you just keep out of it, *Amelia*!" Sophie snaps. "What would you know?"

Mills looks at Sophie in disgust. She hates her real name. Then she says, "Mrs. Piggott, Sophie took your pearls and then tried to frame Amy. I'm so sorry I didn't say something earlier. But Sophie threatened me and —"

"Sophie Piggott," Mrs. Piggott cuts in, her voice icy. "Is this true? Did you take my pearls?"

Sophie's face goes chalk white and then flushes bright red. "No!"

But Mrs. Piggott clearly doesn't believe her. "You did, didn't you? You've always been a terrible liar. I'll kill you! I've warned you before about taking my things and not putting them back. To your room now, before I smack your spoiled little bottom."

Sophie scuttles away and runs toward the house.

Mrs. Piggott says, "I guess I owe you an apology, Amy."

"I guess you do. But you'd better talk to the guards first." Sirens are blaring down the road, and two squad cars with flashing lights pull up outside the house, sending the gravel flying.

Mrs. Piggott tut-tuts. "Oh, dear, I'm in my bathrobe." She tightens the belt around her waist and touches her hair.

"I'd say that's the least of her worries," Clover whispers to me. "They hate false alarms. Let's split."

Mum must have heard Clover's car, because when I try to slip in the back door, she's standing there waiting for me, her arms crossed. She looks furious.

"Amy Green! It's nearly eleven. Where the hell have you been? I've been so worried. I went up to check on you earlier, but you weren't in your room. I thought you'd run away. You'd better have a darned good explanation."

Oops. I should have done the old pillows-under-the-duvet trick. "Sorry, Mum. I was with Clover and Mills. We were at the Piggotts' house. Proving my innocence."

Mum shakes her head. "Oh, Amy, you weren't."

"It's OK; it worked. Clover pretended to be a private investigator and caught Sophie out. It was her all along."

Mum clutches at the back of a chair. "I think I'd better sit down."

When she's sitting at the kitchen table, I tell her the whole story.

Afterward Mum says, "Poor Antonia. She must have felt like a right fool."

"Poor Antonia, my bum. She wanted to ship me off to prison."

Mum smiles. "Anyway, I'm glad it's all ended happily. And you and Mills are obviously friends again?"

I nod. "Speaking of Mills, can she stay the night?" Mills told her mum she was staying the night at Sophie's house. Otherwise she never would have been let out so late. Her overnight bag has been sitting under the garden seat all this time.

"Now?"

I nod again. "She's in the back garden waiting for the all-clear."

"Amy! Oh, go on, bring her in. But don't stay up all night gossiping."

* * *

"I have something to tell you," Mills says at twenty past twelve. "And you might not like it."

We're both lying in my bed. We can't stop talking. We have a lot of catching up to do.

"Look," she says, "I'm just going to say this: I fancy Seth. At least I did."

"What?" I say, genuinely shocked. I stare at her to see if she's joking. But she's not smiling.

She bites her lower lip, and I can see her teeth glowing in the dark. "That's why I was so annoyed with you. I want to tell you everything, be totally honest, so we can start again."

"Seriously?" I ask. "But you said he was a weirdo."

She shrugs and then nods. "I was jealous. Sophie likes him too. She thinks he looks like Johnny Depp."

"No!" I give a laugh. "Ha! This is unbelievable. Wait till I tell him."

"You can't. I'd die."

"Can I at least tell him about Sophie? Please? Seeing as you're not friends with her anymore?"

She bumps her shoulder against mine. "Does that mean we're friends again?"

"I guess so."

"Thanks, Amy."

"For what? Without you and Clover, I'd be banged up in the slammer by now. Because of you, I'm a free woman."

Mills giggles and rolls her eyes. "Stop exaggerating."

"It's good to have you back, Mills."

"You too. Life's far more interesting with you around. Now, tell me all about Seth. Have you kissed him yet?"

♥ Chapter 27

"Antonia rang," Mum says as soon as I walk into the kitchen the following morning. I feel ragged. Mills and I were up till all hours talking, and I'm dog tired and a bit grumpy. She's just gone home.

"She apologized for the whole pearls business. She's grounded Sophie for the rest of the summer. Plus she has to work in the kitchens at the old people's home every morning for free. Anyway, I meant to ask, how did Clover get mixed up in all of this in the first place?"

I smile. "We needed a fast getaway vehicle. . . ."

Mum puts her hands up. "I don't want to know. Trust Clover to get involved. She's worse than you are, Amy."

"At least Clover never doubted me." I look at Dave, who's eating toast and reading the newspaper. "Unlike some."

He looks up. "What? Are you talking about me?"

"Yes, I am actually. You thought I took those pearls. I know you did."

He drops his toast onto the plate, sending crumbs scattering. "That's not fair. I was just trying to back up your mum. And if you look at the facts—"

"The facts?" I glare at him. "Dave, you're supposed to defend me no matter what, not weigh up the evidence. You know, things were a lot easier before you came along. Mum and I were muddling along just fine. Now Mum's a mess, worrying about her marshmallow tummy. And she's exhausted and grumpy all the time."

"Amy!" Mum warns, but I'm on a roll. All my pent-up feelings are coming out—my stress over worrying about the pearls, about the guards and getting arrested, my anxiety over Dad and Shelly, worries about my exam results, which are due any day now.

"You're supposed to be a nurse—you should look after Mum better. All of us better. You've made her paranoid about her figure. And look at the state of you—"

"Amy!" Mum snaps. "That's quite enough. Go to

your room. Immediately." There are angry pink spots on both her cheeks, and her eyes are flashing. I know not to mess with her. I stomp upstairs.

I can hear a heated discussion in the kitchen. The door is closed, but their voices are raised so I can make out most of it. Dave is saying something about how he never asked for any of this. That he's doing his best with me, but I'm not the easiest kid to get along with. That he doesn't know how to handle me most of the time.

Mum's saying it's not her fault, how she had to be good cop and bad cop for ages before he came along, how he can get lost with his judgmental attitude. That I'm right, he's made her a nervous wreck, how the babies are doing her head in, how she wants her old life back. That she just wants everyone to leave her alone for a change.

Then the kitchen door opens, and I can hear every word.

"How can you say that?" Dave demands. "I've given up everything for you, Sylvie. Everything. If you want me to leave, just say the word. I'm *this* close."

"I want you to leave," Mum says. "I think we need to spend some time apart."

And then nothing. Just silence. And seconds later,

bang, the front door slams shut. And Evie starts to cry.

For a split second, I'm glad. But then I realize what's just happened. Dave's gone! He's left Mum. Left all of us. And I made this happen — me and my big mouth. It's all my fault.

♥ *Chapter 28*

A week later and Dave's still not back. Mum told me he's staying with a friend and taking some time out, and that I'm not to worry about it. She said sometimes grown-ups need time and space to think things over.

I also heard her talking to Clover on the phone, saying it was typical — yet again she was the one left holding the babies. And she misses him so much. I think Clover told her just to ask him to come back because then Mum said, "It's not as simple as that. He has to want to come back; he has to want a family and all the messiness that comes with it. And, quite frankly, I don't know if he does."

Clover's been brilliant: she comes over every day to help Mum put the babies to bed. She's pretty hopeless at bathing them or changing nappies, but she sits on the closed toilet seat and watches Mum do it, telling her funny stories about the magazine and making her smile, which is saying a lot.

Dave came over to see the babies on Wednesday, but I was at Mills's house so I missed him. Mum was in an awful state afterward. She was trying to put a brave face on, but I could see she was in bits. She even started crying when Alex threw his pasta at the wall and it left a big puddle-size stain, like one of those ink-blot paintings you do in preschool. Alex is always doing things like that; usually she just laughs and cleans it up. This time I had to deal with it while Mum held the edge of the sink and sobbed.

I feel so guilty, but I don't know what to do. Mum has been moping around the house like a lost soul all week, sighing deeply and gazing out the window as if Dave's about to walk up the path at any moment.

I'm so ashamed, I haven't even told Mills or Seth about what I said to Dave. I'm sure they know something's up; I'm not exactly myself. Clover's been busy at work, so I've been hanging out with Seth and Mills, the three of us.

In the end I didn't tell him about Sophie and Mills fancying him. Mills told me in confidence, and it didn't seem right somehow.

* * *

Dad comes to collect me on Saturday morning, and I'm relieved to get out of the house.

"Is your mum sick?" he asks as we drive away. "She's very quiet." Mum's standing in the doorway, gazing at the back of Dad's car. It's eleven and she's still in her pajamas with an old sweatshirt of Dave's pulled over them. "Is she still upset about the whole baby thing?"

"No. Dave's gone," I say simply.

"*What?*" Dad almost crashes into the car in front. He signals and then pulls over. He turns and looks at me, his face full of shock and concern. "Why? What happened?"

"They had a fight." Tears prick the back of my eyes. "Dad, what am I going to do? It's all my fault."

"Of course it's not your fault." Dad strokes my head. "I'm sure it's just a silly argument that adults have."

"No, it *is* my fault." I tell him exactly what happened. And give him his due, he doesn't contradict me.

"I can see why you think that," he says. "But there was obviously something simmering away underneath. Dave's a decent guy. He wouldn't just leave because of one thing you said to him. But I know the two of you don't exactly see eye to eye. Have you been making things difficult for him in general, Amy?"

I think for a moment. Maybe I have made life hard for Dave. Shelly too. I have a huge lump in my throat, so I just shrug glumly.

"Sometimes life isn't easy for any of us," Dad says gently. "You should give him a chance. He makes your mum happy. And that's the only thing that matters, isn't it?"

I start crying. "Yes," I say through my tears. But what about me? Don't I count too? I swipe my tears away with the back of my hand. I just want to be on my own. "Dad, can I go home? Do you mind?"

"Not at all. Shelly will be disappointed, though. She's decorated the attic for you. She found an Italian sofa in Arnotts, and she's ordered new curtains to match. And she bought you a new flat-screen telly and a DVD player. All out of her own money."

"Must have cost her."

"She insisted. After all that business with the baby's room and everything. She really wants the two of you to be friends."

"Friends?" I make a face.

"Amy! Just try to be nice to her. She'll need your help once the baby's here. She doesn't have any sisters or anything. You're all she's got."

I take a deep breath. *Be big*, I tell myself. *Don't go*

messing up yet again. "Tell her she can ring me. But only in an emergency."

He smiles at me gratefully. "Thanks, Amy."

Dad drops me off at the end of the road, but instead of walking home, I hop on the train to Gramps's house. It's not far to walk, but I can't wait. I desperately need to talk to Clover.

"Hi, Beanie," Clover says as she opens the door. "I was hoping it was you. I need your help. I got this e-mail about kissing—"

"I have to find Dave," I tell her frantically. "It's urgent."

"Is he still AWOL?" she asks.

I nod. "I have to talk to him. He has to come home. Mum's miserable without him. And no one's taken out the bin all week. There are these horrible little flies hovering over the box for the compost, and the nappy bin is so full Mum and I can't lift it. The whole house stinks."

Clover starts to laugh.

"Why are you laughing?" I demand. "It's not funny!"

"You want Dave back 'cause the house smells?"

"No! Not just that. Mum misses him. And the babies miss him."

She looks at me, her head tilted to one side. "And what about you, Beanie? Do you miss him?"

"A little," I admit. "But most of all I miss Mum. She's not herself at the moment. It's like living with someone out of *Coronation Street*. She never stops crying, and she's been wearing her bathrobe all week. She hasn't had a shower for days. She'll be smoking next and drinking gin at breakfast. I can't take it anymore."

"So you want to convince him to come home?"

"Yes, if I can."

"Then there's something you should read first. It might just help you understand where he's coming from. I found it a while back when I was Googling a fashion label called Colts."

"That's Dave's old band, isn't it? The Colts?"

"It sure is, Beanie. He's so obvious. Wait there." She walks out the back door and into her office. She comes back out with a plastic folder in her hands. Then she grabs her car keys from the pottery bowl on the hall table. "What are we waiting for? Let's go. You can read this in the car."

"But where will we find him? I don't know where he's staying."

She looks at me crookedly. "Amy, you've been solving problems with me for weeks now. Use your head." She knocks on my head gently with her knuckles. "We're going to the hospital."

"Why didn't I think of that?"

"Because clearly I have the superior brain."

As Clover parks the car in the Saint Vincent's car park, my stomach is in knots. What am I going to say to him? What if he won't talk to me? What if he's not on duty at all? I know he's on days at the moment because I rang Mum on the way over here — she was so spaced out, she didn't even ask why I wanted to know — but maybe his rotation has changed.

"Stop worrying, Beanie," Clover says as she locks the car. "It'll be fine. Just tell him what you told me. Without mentioning the trash bins."

I nod silently, still feeling sick.

I know where the nurses' station is because I've come in before with Mum. As we approach, I see Dave sitting inside, reading a patient's chart. He looks tired, his face is pale, and he has dark rings under his eyes. Sensing my gaze, he looks up and our eyes lock. He says something to the nurse beside him and walks toward me. I can feel my cheeks burn. I still have no idea what I'm going to say.

"I'll be just down the corridor," Clover says quietly.

"No, stay," I say, but she's already gone.

"Amy," Dave says. It's hard to read the expression on his face. He has every right to be annoyed with me, but he doesn't seem angry. "What are you doing here?"

I open my mouth to say something, but nothing comes out.

"Did your mum send you?" he asks.

I shake my head. "No. It was my idea. Clover drove me here. I just want to talk to you."

"So talk."

I look around, floundering. Why is this so difficult? *Just say sorry,* I tell myself. *Apologize for being mean to him. Ask him to come home.*

"Mum misses you," I manage.

"Does she, now?"

"And the babies. Alex won't sleep on his own. He's been in Mum's bed all week."

Dave makes a tiny clicking noise with his tongue against his teeth, and I realize what I've said. "*Your* bed," I correct myself.

"That's just it." He sighs. "Look, this whole family thing is bigger than I am." He runs his hands over his head. "I don't know if I can do it. Do you understand?"

I shrug. The thing is, after what I read in the car, I

think I do understand. But I don't know how to put it into words.

Dave says, "I'm sorry, Amy. I have to go back to work. Take care of yourself." He starts to walk back toward the nurses' station.

Just then Clover appears beside me. "Go after him." She gives me a serious look. "Go on. It might be your last chance. Be brave, Beanie. Talk to him."

I feel a wave of panic. "I can't."

She looks at me again, her lips pressed together in a thin line. "Your call. But if you don't, you're not the girl I thought you were."

I have a lump the size of a golf ball in my throat, and I feel like crying. I can't bear to disappoint Clover.

OK, Amy. You have two choices here. You can let Dave walk away, or you can try and fix things. Which are you going to do?

"Dave!" I yell down the hall, running after him. "Wait. I've read your blog. I understand."

♥ Chapter 29

"What?" Dave's eyes slide away from mine and rest on the clipboard in his hands. Then he recovers himself. "I don't have a blog, Amy. When would I get the time?"

"When you're on nights. There's wi-fi in the coffee shop, and you use your laptop." It's a long shot, but from the look of surprise on Dave's face, I can tell I'm right.

"That doesn't prove anything."

"Dave, it's called 'Diary of a Tamed Colt.' Like your old band. *And* my friend has traced the blog to your laptop. He's a computer genius." Now this isn't strictly true, but Clover said Brains could do this if we asked him to.

But it's enough to make Dave tuck his clipboard under his arm, put his hands out in front of him, and say, "Arrest me, officer. I'll come quietly. But I didn't know blogging was a crime, honest. Look, can we talk about this somewhere more private?" He points at a door. "In here. Edna won't mind."

I look around for Clover, but she's disappeared. I follow him into the room. An old woman with a pink face as wrinkly as a prune is snoring soundly in one of the beds. Curtains are drawn around the other bed.

"Don't worry, that one's empty," Dave says. "The patient's gone home. And Edna would sleep through anything, wouldn't you, Edna?" She gives a fruity snore.

"So how much of my blog have you read?" he asks. He leans his back against the window ledge.

I shrug. "Just a few bits." Clover had printed out his profile and some posts she thought I'd find interesting. I'd forgotten Dave was younger than Mum: thirty-one. Almost as young as Shelly. It felt very strange reading his private thoughts. But they were up on the Internet for the whole world to read, so I didn't feel all that bad.

Diary of a Tamed Colt

ABOUT ME

AGE: 31
GENDER: male
LOCATION: Dublin, Ireland
PROFESSION: Nurse. I used to be a singer/songwriter
MARITAL STATUS: Living with my partner, one moody teenager, and two noisy babies

December 8

BABIES

Yesterday I held my sister's three-week-old baby, Bella. She wriggled around in my arms and let out an amazingly loud fart before filling her nappy with the most poisionous-smelling mustard goo with bits swimming around in it. It looked like scrambled eggs. (I know because my sister changed her in front of me — disgusting!) I felt exactly nothing for this baby, even though she's my niece. Nothing!

I'm seriously worried. Our own baby is due in a few months. What if I feel nothing for it?

I'm scared. What if I'm a useless dad?

259 ♥

February 20

TEENAGE SCREAM-AGE

I don't understand teenage girls. One minute she's perfectly normal; the next minute she's morphed into some kind of Valkyrie warrior queen from hell. I'm doing my best, but it never seems to be good enough. Are all teenage girls crazy?

Am I supposed to discipline her, be strict? Am I supposed to be her friend?

March 14

WHERE HAS MY LIFE GONE?

One day I'm an up-and-coming singer/songwriter, and the next I'm back at the day (and night) job. What happened?

I feel like my dreams have all gone down the toilet because I have to pay all the bills. Do you have any idea how much nappies cost? Or teenagers' clothes?

I feel so frustrated. There are all these song ideas running around in my head, but when I get home, I'm too tired to write. There are always babies to walk or nursery rhymes to sing.

I'm only thirty-one. Why do I feel so old?

"I'm sorry." He looks sheepish. "I didn't think any-one I knew would actually read it. I was just blowing off steam. Though I suppose using the word 'Colt' was pretty obvious."

"Did you mean all that stuff about not feeling anything for Bella?"

"Yes, at the time. But it's different when it's your own baby. It's all about genetics. You have a special bond right from the start."

I give a snort.

He stops and looks at me. "OK, Amy, you want the truth — here's the truth: Babies are easy. You kiss them; they don't push you away. You love them, and they love you right back, unconditionally. But you're different. You've always blown hot and cold with me. At the start we got on great. I taught you how to play 'Yellow Submarine' on the guitar, remember? We used to dance around the kitchen together.

"But when Alex was born and you went to stay with Gramps and Clover, you came back a different person. I tried to hug you, and you pushed me away. And that hasn't really changed, has it?" He laughs bitterly. "I can't compete with Art. Big-shot trader with the fancy car and the exotic holidays. He still owns half the house. How do you think that makes me feel?"

"Big-shot trader who ran off with his secretary," I remind him. "Big-shot trader who forgot my birthday last year until Mum reminded him. And now you've run off too."

"I haven't run off!" Dave looks horrified. "It's not as simple as that."

"Come home, then."

"I can't."

"Why? Mum's so upset. She can't sleep, and she hasn't eaten for days. Please? She misses you. And the babies miss you too. Alex was looking under the kitchen table for you last night."

"And what about *you*? Do you miss me?"

I open my mouth to say something, but he says quickly, "You don't have to answer that. You see, Amy, it's different with you. You're not my biological daughter, but I choose to love you. I can't help it. You're a great kid. And I'm sorry if I don't tell you that often enough. The way you help with the babies and everything. If you left the house instead of me, then things really would fall apart."

This time I think before I open my mouth. "I'm sorry if I've pushed you away. But I was ten when I met you. I'm thirteen now. Of course I've changed. I'm a teenager! I don't hug Dad much, either. And

I've never hugged Shelly, not once. So please, stop with the hugging!

"And you don't have to be strict, either. Just be yourself: Dave Marcus. The dad *and* the musician. You can be both, you know. And in a few years, Evie and Alex can be your backup singers. Why don't you write something for them instead of all those 'Woe is me, life's rubbish, and I'm going to die' songs you used to write?"

"Thanks a million, Amy." He's grinning so I know he hasn't taken offense. "And that's not a bad idea. Rock songs for kids. You might have something there." He pauses. "Do you really want me back?"

"Yes! We *all* miss you. Please. Just come home."

The curtains around the empty bed swish open, and Clover jumps out.

She says, "That's sorted, then. Everyone's happy and, Dave, you're going to be Ireland's answer to the Doodlebops or the Wiggles."

"Clover!" Dave says. "I've just made that bed."

She just smiles. "Love the blog, by the way. Ever thought of journalism?"

"I'm taking it down as soon as I can get to a computer." Dave narrows his eyes. "Who else knows about it? Did you tell Sylvie, Clover?"

"Nope," she says. "And my lips are sealed."

"Mine too," I promise. "As long as you come home, that is."

"Hey! That's blackmail," Dave says.

Clover grins. "I've taught her everything she knows."

♥ Epilogue

Later, when I tell Mum that Dave's coming home for good, and that he'll be back as soon as his shift's over, she staggers toward the kitchen table, flops down on a chair, and begins to howl into her hands. Not the reaction I'd expected.

"Thank God," she says after a few minutes, her voice still rough and hiccupy from the crying. Her nose is running, and her eyes are pink and puffy. "What a relief." She brushes away her tears with the sleeve of her bathrobe. Then she stands up and gives me a hug, getting snot all over my T-shirt, but I don't mind.

"Amy, I don't know what you said to him, but thank you. You're amazing."

She's making me a bit nervous. "Can I go over to Clover's now? She's waiting for me."

"Of course. But can you watch the babies for a few minutes first? I think I'd better take a shower."

After I've filled Clover in, she rubs her hands together and says, "Excellent! Now, let's get back to business. I need some help with this kissing e-mail. . . . Poor girl's worried about teeth clashing, but it's perfectly normal. Happens all the time." She looks up at me, a glint in her eye. "Tell me exactly what you need to know, *Samantha*."

"Clover!" I blush. "It's not me."

"'Course it's not, Beanie. But who else would give me an idea for an article, complete with a perfect title?"

I smile and listen to her intently as she gives me step-by-step instructions. After all, my summer break has begun. Three months of freedom — hurrah for long Irish school holidays! Mills is my best friend again, Dave's back to do the bins, and I have a fab boyfriend. With a bit of luck, I might get to try out Clover's advice any day now. Things are looking up!

P.S. I passed all my exams.

P.P.S. I got an A in math. The only bad comment on my report card was from Mr. Olen: "If Amy spent as much time drawing as she does talking to a certain male class member, she'd be a future Leonardo da Vinci."

Glossary

Hi,

Amy here.

I live in Ireland, which is a pretty weird place at the best of times. So I've jotted down some notes to help you understand what I'm on about! ♥

agony aunt: Most teen mags in Ireland and the UK have an "agony aunt"— a journalist or relationship expert who answers the readers' problem letters. The letters and the answers are printed on the mag's pages. Some mags have several agony aunts — relationship ones, medical ones. Some even have an agony uncle, to give an insight into the murky minds of males! Clover is the agony aunt for the *Goss* mag, and I get to help her — cool, huh?

Bebo: A social networking site. A bit like MySpace — you can add YouTube clips, songs, and pics, plus chat with your friends.

clobber: Clothes. Can also mean to hit someone, as in "He clobbered me." But generally used to mean what you're wearing!

Crombies: Boys, usually, but not exclusively rugby players, who wear American labels like Abercrombie & Fitch or American Eagle. They say "ledge" a lot (short for *legend*), as in "Charlie's so cool — he's a ledge with the girls." Yes, folks, they are the nearest we have in Ireland to Neanderthal men. And of course, D4s find them wildly attractive — figures! Kind of like American jocks, I guess.

D4s: Mean girls who live in or aspire to live in Dublin 4, a posh area of the city. D4 is a post code, or zip code for you guys. They wear Ugg boots, skinny jeans or minis, and are addicted to fake tan and straightening their dyed hair. They love shopping and have a passionate love affair with their mobiles. "OMG" is their fave expression. Bullying is second nature to them — it's in their designer jeans — sorry, genes. They are, in general, a sad bunch and to be pitied.

Dermot O'Leary: Dermot is the host of the UK's talent-search show, *The X Factor*. So think Ryan Seacrest, but with edgier suits (sorry, Ryan!).

Drummies: D4 girls who hang around in packs in a huge shopping center in Dundrum, a Dublin suburb. They clearly have nothing better to do, folks!

Dubes: Dubarry deck shoes; de rigueur for Crombies and other rugger buggers.

Dundrum: Ireland's biggest and snazziest shopping center — mall to you. Has its own fountain and everything. Mecca of the D4s (Drummies) and Yummy Mummies alike.

Dun Laoghaire: You say it "Dun Leery." Hard-to-pronounce but pretty cool seaside town near Dublin city.

eejit: Idiot/nerd/dork to those in the U.S. of Amazing! Can also be used as a verb — as in "Would you stop eejiting around, Amy?"

emos: People, usually teenagers, who are into "emotive hardcore music" such as My Chemical Romance and I Would Set Myself on Fire for You (yes, this really is the name of a band, folks). Emos wear a lot of black and are very attached to their black Converse boots (high-tops to you), the more scuffed and beaten up the better. Or checked Vans. They also love black eyeliner — girls *and* boys. I must admit I have a bit of a soft spot for them — until they all start making cartoon kissing noises and hugging each other — now, that's just plain weird.

Gordon D'Arcy, Brian O'Driscoll, and Ronan O'Gara: Very attractive Irish rugby players with legs to die for. Especially in muddy rugby shorts.

guards: The Irish police force is called An Garda Síochána, which means "the peace guard." We call them guards for short or the Gardaí. Not that I've had any dealings with them, you understand. Now, Clover, that's a different matter. . . .

Mark Rothko: A dead Russian-American artist who painted huge, side-of-a-bus-size abstract canvases (which really means they have no people or things in them, just colors and shapes). They are *amazing*. Looking at them is like falling into a big pool of color and emotion. He's Seth's fave artist, one of mine too. Along with Georgia O'Keeffe, who lived in a desert and mainly painted sheep skulls and ginormous flowers. She's also dead.

Oh, My Goddesses: Another name for Drummies or D4s.

OMG: Abbreviation of "Oh, my God" (pronounced "Eoi, moi Gawd" in D4 speak).

Penneys: Irish clothes chain—home of way-cheap clothes and fashion savior of many a teenage girl, *moi* included. Kind of like H&M or Topshop.

siúcra: Means sugar in Irish. Pronounced "shoe-kra."

siúcra ducra: Clover made this up—it just means double sugar!

snog: A kiss—but more than a peck on the cheek ;). Can also be used as a verb: "Did you snog him, Amy?" or "I saw the pair of you snogging the faces off each other."

spondulicks: Money. We use euros in Ireland, which is handy if you want to travel—most countries in Europe are fully euro-ed up now!

Turn the page for an excerpt from

Ask Amy Green

SUMMER SECRETS

♥ Chapter 1

"It's soooo unfair," I moan, my head on Seth's lap. We're lying on Killiney Beach, our special place. Seth's my boyfriend (I love saying that — boyfriend!), and it was on this very beach that I first noticed his amazing sky-blue eyes, not to mention his washboard stomach. His dog, Billy, is rolling around in the sand beside us, yapping happily.

Seth winds my hair around his fingers. "I know, but it's only three weeks."

"*Only* three weeks? A lot can happen in three weeks."

We've only been together for nine weeks. So if you look at it that way, three weeks is a very long time — 33.3 (recurring) percent of our relationship, to be exact. Sorry, I like math. Geeky, I know, but a girl has to have her vices!

I'm off on holiday with my crazy family — all of them. And when your parentals are divorced, like mine, and both have new partners, that's a lot of people. Dave — my mum's boyfriend — has even invited his posh sister and her family along too.

The shared family holiday was Dad's idea. He claimed it would be a bonding experience for everyone after certain recent events — but it sounds like a nightmare to me. Luckily, Clover, my seventeen-year-old aunt, is coming along too. Otherwise I'd go mad.

And get this: while I'm stuck in Cork for two weeks on the holiday from hell, Seth's off for three weeks to a big farmhouse just outside Rome. They're flying out this evening. His mum, Polly, is teaching photography at this arty-farty place that sounds like a weirdie commune to me — all hippy-dippy veggie food and workshops on connecting with your inner child. (Are they serious? Who'd want to do that?)

Seth is smiling down at me, his blond hair flopping over his eyes. There's a new smattering of cute sun freckles over the bridge of his nose. "I'll write to you," he says.

"E-mail, you mean."

"That too. But I meant pen and paper. Envelope, stamp, the works."

"Why would you do that? It's a lot of hassle. Do they even have post boxes in the wilds of Italia?"

He shrugs. "I like letters." The tops of his ears have flared a little and he looks away. "But e-mail is fine," he says quietly.

Poor Seth, he probably has his letters all planned out. He's a bit of a Boy Scout sometimes: likes to be prepared. Maybe he was thinking of sending me some sketches too. He's brilliant at art. And now I've gone and squashed his idea.

"No, you're right," I say. "Let's write proper letters."

"Cool." He stops for a moment before adding, "As long as you can read my handwriting." His mouth twists a little. "And I can't spell, either."

I've been wondering about this for a while. His texts are full of spelling mistakes. "Are you dyslexic?" I ask.

He shrugs. "I guess. I went to this psychologist, and I had to have extra reading and spelling classes in primary school, but Mum doesn't want to make a big deal of it. I wanted to drop out of Irish, but she wouldn't let me. You need it to work for RTÉ. She rang and asked them."

"RTÉ?" (Radio Telefis Éireann is Ireland's national telly and radio station. Like the BBC.) "You want to be an actor?" I grab a piece of driftwood and start singing "Summer Nights" into it. The school drama club is doing *Grease* in September. Mills and I are determined to be in it, mainly 'cause it means: one, skipping a double Irish class on a Friday afternoon for rehearsals, and, two, meeting cute older boys. I have Seth, of course, but Mills is dying to meet someone, and she likes her boys "mature."

Seth would make a brilliant Danny if only I could persuade him to audition. He's not exactly Mr. School and barely goes to all his classes as it is. I can see him now, though, up on the stage, hair slicked back, leather jacket, tight black jeans, his slim hips wiggling — oh, baby!

"Earth calling Amy; come in, Amy." Seth is staring at me.

My eyes are resting on his hips, and I drag them away. How embarrassing! I cover my pink cheeks with my hands. "I think I've had a bit too much sun," I say. "Sorry, what were you saying about the telly?"

"Radio. I want to work in radio."

"As a DJ?"

"No. Behind the scenes. Production or research."

Just then my mobile beeps. I read the text message:

AMY, HOME NOW! U MUST PACK. R U STILL AT
CLOVER'S? UR MOTHER!

"Oops," I say, climbing to my feet and brushing
sand off my bum. I haven't even been to Clover's
yet.

Seth puts his arms around my waist and tries to
pull me back down onto the sand.

I shriek. "Unhand me, Casanova."

"It'll cost you." He grins up at me. "A kiss."

My tummy does a flip. Clover's comprehensive
kissing lessons are certainly coming in useful. He
loosens his grip on my waist. I put one leg on either
side of his and sit on his lap; then, leaning forward,
I tilt my head a little. Our lips connect. *Zing!* There
goes the electricity again, radiating out from my lips;
within seconds, my whole body feels tingly. I open
my mouth a bit and feel the warm tip of his tongue
against mine. Then—

Yap, yap, yap. Billy barks in my ear and jumps on
my back.

I break away from Seth, startled. "Ow." I rub my
skin through my T-shirt. He has sharp claws.

"Bad dog," Seth tells Billy, pulling him away from
me by his collar. I give my mouth a quick wipe with
the back of my hand.

When Billy has finally calmed down, Seth says, "Sorry about that. I don't know what's wrong with him today."

My mobile starts to ring. It's Mum. Double oops.

"Angry parental alert. I really have to skedaddle. I'll text you the address of the holiday house. And the landline." I groan. "Two weeks of hell."

He shrugs. "It might be fun."

I pull a face. "Yeah, right. But at least Clover's going — that's something."

Seth grins. "She's a bad influence. Stay out of jail. And Amy?"

"Yes?"

"I'll miss you."

Acknowledgments

Muchos, muchos thanks to: My long-suffering partner and children — Ben, Amy, Jago, and most especially Sam, my Bebo and music adviser. My fab sisters, Kate and Emma; and Mum and Dad, for all the babysitting.

My best friends, Tanya and Nicky. We've been friends for over twenty years now (scary thought!), and they're still talking to me, which is a minor miracle. And special thanks to Tanya for keeping me on the fashion straight and narrow. I'd still be in puffball dresses and rah-rah skirts if it wasn't for her (but they're probably back in by now!).

My wonderful writer in crime, Martina Devlin, who puts up with me going on and on about my plots and characters. And to all my writer friends in the Irish Girls and Irish PEN.

And, of course, I must mention the incredible team at Walker Books: my eagle-eyed and wise editor, Gill Evans; Jane Harris, who made Amy Green happen in the first place; the very talented Annalie Grainger, an editor who really keeps you on your toes; the lovely and always smiley Jo Humphreys-Davies; agony aunt extraordinaire, Alice Burden; Katie Everson, for the fab design and cover; and all the fantastic sales team, most especially my own Irish champion, Conor Hackett. And to the fab team at Candlewick Press: Sarah Ketchersid and her editorial team for all their hard work on the manuscript and Karen Lotz for saying such lovely things about Amy and Clover.

I must also thank my new agents, Philippa and Peta at L.A.W. for all their support. Plus my very first reader and adviser, Kate Gordon, for all her hard work. Kate read the

Boy Trouble manuscript several times and said such lovely things about it in the early stages that I just had to keep going.

To my other teen (and almost teen) editorial readers — Laura, Astrid, Annie, Naoise, and Sinéad — for saying such nice things about the book.

And a big thanks to all my great friends in children's bookselling: children's guru at Eason, Dave O'Callaghan, for the guyliner inspiration and the CDs; Amanda Dalton; honorary member of the children's book fraternity Susan Walsh; and all the children's buyers at Dubray Books, for their support and encouragement.

To Liz Morris for her editorial insight and her friendship and Mary Byrne for all her help. And to fellow writers Cathy Hopkins, Judi Curtin, and Marita Conlon-McKenna for their lovely feedback.

To the dedicated and fun team at Children's Books Ireland, and fellow children's booksellers everywhere — keep the faith, folks!

And finally to you, the reader. Thank you so much for picking up this book. I'd love to hear from you, so please do contact me via Facebook:

www.facebook.com/sarahwebbwriter

or via my website:

www.askamygreen.com,

or you can e-mail me directly:

sarah@askamygreen.com.

I'll get back to you as quickly as I can! Or write via my publishers: Candlewick Press, 99 Dover Street, Somerville, MA 02144.

Best wishes,
Sarah XXX